Praise for

The Usual Suspects

"Readers will love watching these two uniquely gifted black boys explore the complicated tensions between impulses and choices, independence and support, turnin' up and getting through."
—*Kirkus Reviews* (starred review)

"A rare and much-needed glimpse into the world of exceptional learners."
—*School Library Journal*

"Broaddus sheds revealing light on the nature of systemic profiling based on class, race, and neurodiversity, at schools and within society."
—*Publishers Weekly*

"Through its discerning, young Black protagonist, *The Usual Suspects* tackles difficult subjects with nuance, humor, and heart, always bringing it back to the characters. A great choice for upper middle graders in search of a fun and meaningful read."
—ALA *Booklist*

the USUAL SUSPECTS

MAURICE BROADDUS

 KATHERINE TEGEN BOOKS

An Imprint of HarperCollins Publishers

For Reese

Library of Congress Control Number: 2018962176
ISBN 978-0-06-279632-5

Typography by Laura Eckes
22 23 24   PC/BRR   10 9 8 7 6 5 4 3
❖
First paperback edition, 2020

the USUAL SUSPECTS

Life is all about timing.

Once the homeroom bell rings at 8:15 a.m., there'll be a five-minute lag before students are marched to the auditorium to gather for morning assembly. Nehemiah Caldwell and I get there before any administration types do. We slide under the curtain beneath the stage and crawl over to the stereo cart.

This is going to be epic.

"You got it?" Nehemiah asks.

I pat my pocket. "Yeah. You got what you need?"

"I'm like a Boy Scout up in this mug." He

untangles wires from a box with computer ports in it. He then begins to draw the cord, pulling the cart closer to us.

"Easy, easy . . ."

"If you think this is so easy, you come do this."

"Shh! She might hear you." I scoot over and help pull on the cord. We draw the cart until it's pressed against the stage. The music teacher's absent today; his mistake was announcing it in advance. Since he runs sound for morning assembly, he preset the mixing board so that all the person filling in for him had to do was hit the power button.

We have other plans.

"Can you reach the laptop?" Nehemiah asks.

"Let me make sure it's clear." I pop my head out. The new principal, Mrs. Fitzgerald, talks to a teacher at the far entrance, her back to us. I study the folks I'm going up against. Mrs. Fitzgerald has a swagger to her. A bit of a gangster vibe. She wanders the halls with a beaming smile, but she has a resting teacher face with her eyes narrow like unflinching lasers. Most kids fear crossing her. But I don't.

2

I snatch the laptop and hope no one was paying attention.

"Got it," I say.

"Hand me the flash drive."

"Here you go." I crouch back, giving the man space to work.

Nehemiah's unaware that he sticks his tongue out like he's about to dunk a basketball. Playing ball, playing video games, or him in front of a computer are the only times he gets his game face on. "All right, that should do it."

"You sure?"

"You want to keep questioning me, or you wanna get ghost before we get caught?"

We scramble out the back way, popping up near the stairs on the far side of the stage. As we're about to dip out, our teacher Mr. Blackmon rounds the corner.

"Fellas." Mr. Blackmon nods, checking us out as he does so. "Where are you supposed to be?"

"Homeroom," we say in angelic choir unison.

"Better hurry then. Tardy bell's about to ring."

We arrive at our classroom just in time to be first in line to march down to the auditorium for assembly. We sit in front where everyone can keep their eyes on us. Mrs. Fitzgerald walks toward center stage. Once she starts moving, the entire school snaps to attention, like her shadow passing over us is enough to freeze us in our spots.

"Good morning," she says, but the microphones are dead so only the first few rows hear her. Tapping the mike with her long fingernails, she gestures to the sound board.

I sit, stiff and quiet, all but grabbing Nehemiah's hand in anticipation of the moment.

The sub hits the power button.

Over Nehemiah's beatboxing, my rhymes spit over the school speakers.

You missed the orientation so you can't school me.
I keep my mind right so you can't fool me.
Sitting 'round judging me like I'm brand-new
Call me infamous, felonius, the one true boo.
My moms, she's a queen raising a young king,

Told me to chase my dreams, grow up, and do
    my thing.
Ain't no stopping me 'cause you know I get
    lawless when you get in my way
Trying to make it out here 'cause they hating on
    me I'm a-let them boys say
A little kid standing tall
You in my world and I want it all.

The kids erupt. They can't sing along since it's my original, but they can bob their heads and cheer. Since the administration types couldn't figure out how to stop the vocals, they cut the power to the sound board. Which is too bad, because my rhymes were just getting to the good part.

So I'm back in the principal's office once again. Due to "my escalating antics" I'm here a lot. Some teachers float the idea that I have oppositional defiant disorder (sometimes I think they just say that about kids who say no whenever adults tell them to do something, in which case, I have a severe case of it, as does every middle schooler I know). Some keep trying to say that I have bipolar disorder (because my shenanigans are so over-the-top). None of them are a doctor. They just want to sweep me and my issues under the rug. Moms scheduled an exam for me to get tested, but with our insurance, it's over a month out. Until then, I have to spend the rest of the quarter in the Special Ed room.

School policy is to deposit all their troublemakers or kids who they think are too much for a teacher to handle—no matter what grade—into one classroom. "Warehoused" is the word they were searching for. All their problem children, labeled "emotionally delinquent," putting "the ED in education," our homeroom teacher Mrs. Horner once joked. They say we're too "disruptive"—I can almost see them make air quotes like they want to call us something else—like we're some disease they're trying to isolate.

I figure because she's so young and new, Mrs. Fitzgerald feels like she has a lot to prove. Plus every new principal wants things done their way. Partly to show there's a new sheriff in town, partly to shake things up. Every new teacher or principal has it in their head that they're going to fix everything. Especially us. It's like we're lab rats in some kind of science experiment. Too bad I've never had a taste for cheese.

"Thelonius Mitchell, you spend so much time on that bench they should name it after you," Mrs. Carson says. She's the head of hospitality, office manager, and school nurse.

"I'm sure it's all a misunderstanding." I take my seat.

"It always is with you." She shakes her head and continues her work.

I put on my best innocent face, my thick braids flopping like a mophead when I tilt my chin. Now is one of those times I wish I wore glasses. I have a theory that people always trust folks who wear glasses more. I begin to tick off the things I may or may not have done wrong since the assembly incident that might have come back to bite me:

- removing all the toilet paper from the adult restrooms

- borrowing my homeroom teacher's credit card so I could pay for online poker

- locking the girls' locker room after releasing a half-dozen mice in there

To be fair, I am only in the planning stages of swiping the snack baskets from the middle school breakfast (getting them isn't the problem, nor is getting them out the building an issue once I divert the security camera near the back stairwell. Sneaking them home is the real stumbling block).

Now that I think about it, I should probably wear about six pairs of glasses at all times.

"Well, well, well. Look who we have here. If it isn't *Felonius*." Marcel Washington slips out of the principal's office and closes the door behind her as if she owns the place. She wears black and brown tortoiseshell glasses. Now *those* are some trust builders. No wonder teachers adore her. She wears her hair straight and sashays about like she just wakes up every morning with every strand in place. She also has her momma's fair skin. A lone brown freckle dots her lip just above her smirk. "I guess it's no surprise . . . considering."

"Considering what?" I arch an eyebrow at her. Marcel always has a tone in her voice like she knows something you don't, but she wants you to know that she knows.

"Mrs. Fitzgerald will tell you."

"You in trouble, too?"

"Too? You must have me confused with one of your fellow knuckleheads. I was called down to be put in charge of the student ambassadors. You're here because you're . . . you." She nudges her glasses higher up her nose with her index finger. She has a way of looking at everyone as if they are small.

"We ain't that different." I shrug, determined not to let her get under my skin.

"Sure we are. You get caught." Marcel winks.

I hate it when she winks. It's worse than her smirk.

She walks down the hallway, twirling her hall pass, reminding me of how much I can't stand her. No one can see how much of a lady gangster she is because she's an honor student. Student ambassadors often help school staff with little jobs like recording attendance. Because of that, one of the many services Marcel "offers" is covering your skipped classes by making sure you're marked as present. I hate having to deal with her, but she and her crew control all the action in the school. So us independent operators of mischief sometimes don't have a choice.

Mrs. Fitzgerald's door opens enough for her to pop her head out. She does not have her play face on. "Come on in, Mr. Mitchell."

The walk from your cell to the electric chair is the longest walk in your life.

This is Mrs. Fitzgerald's first couple of months as principal of Persons Crossing Public Academy. Mrs. Horner still complains about her being the youngest principal in the district because "these young people don't understand how the world works." I really think Mrs. Horner is just mad because Mrs. Fitzgerald replaced one of those old-school principals who Mrs. Horner liked. The first words out of that principal's mouth was always "Back in my day." Old School never talked to anyone, just shouted at them. I might as well have been a wall. But Mrs. Fitzgerald is different. She might be tough and take no nonsense, but she listens when we talk.

When I sink into the chair nearest her desk, I say, "I didn't do it."

"Funny how you just assume that you must've done something wrong in order to find yourself in my office," she says.

Despite her all-business face, Mrs. Fitzgerald has a natural prettiness to her. Not that I think she is pretty. It's just that up close, I can't tell if she even wears makeup. She has a long angular face, smooth skin, and flowing black hair she brushes out of her eyes whenever she focuses on whoever she speaks to. Especially me. Her stare makes me feel like I'm under a microscope. Still, part of me finds it nice to know that someone who looks like my mother is in charge.

I shift in discomfort. "Didn't I?"

"Mr. Mitchell." She loves to add "Mr." or "Miss" to our names to demonstrate respect toward us. It throws us off every time, but it's kind of okay, too. "I make it a point to know as many children at my school as possible. There are two kinds of kids whose names I learn first: my honor students and my problem students. I learned your name before any teacher had a chance to even hand out their first homework assignment of the year."

"I get good grades." I pick up a pencil and start twirling it between my fingers.

"If that's all there was to learning, you wouldn't need the support of special education. Do you remember how we met?"

Adults think they're slick the way they use words like they're fooling someone. Like how when they say "high energy" or "impulse control issues," it's code for ADHD. Or like when they say "support" they might as well mean "punish."

"That was nearly a third of my lifetime ago." It was back in fourth grade. She was a vice principal then, in charge of school discipline. But those were my lower school days. In middle school, you had a new slate.

"You're a clever boy. In fact, have you ever heard the expression 'too clever by half'? That's you."

"This is an awful lot of math for me being in trouble. Fractions were never my strongest subject."

"There's that cleverness again. I think we've had about enough of it for today." Even at her sternest, a smile usually dances in her eyes to let kids know that she still cares about them. But if it's possible for her to have even *less* play in her face, Mrs. Fitzgerald managed it.

Something is stressing her out for real, but she isn't about to reveal her hand until she's ready. Now I ain't scared of anyone, but I know now might not be the best time to mess around. I fold my hands in my lap to avoid the temptation of them fumbling into something they shouldn't.

"You're bright and have a lot of potential. I hate to see people squander their potential. Do you know what 'squander' means?"

"Yes, ma'am." Every opportunity to have a teaching moment she takes. It must be in their handbook or something.

"Ah, here comes the rest of your classmates." Mrs. Fitzgerald waves in the faces pressed against her door window.

Nehemiah dips his head in first as if checking to see if the coast is clear. We're both in the seventh grade. Compared to him, I'm sculpted like an Olympian. He seems built like a collection of angry twigs. His skin is almost as dark as the black jacket he always wears. Our school dress code is red or navy polo shirts with navy or khaki pants (girls have an option for skirts). Since he always complains about being cold, teachers letting him wear it was better than the alternative. Nehemiah has a way of . . . melting down when he gets overwhelmed. And by "melting down" I mean screaming and running through the halls.

Next in is Twon. His full name is Antoine Beverly after an uncle he hates, so he goes by Twon. A big kid, even for an eighth grader. His breath always smells like beef jerky and bubble gum. His red shirt, now almost pink from repeated washing, is tucked into his pants. The knees are worn down to threads. The school powers that be intended the official school uniform to equalize fashion among the students. So that kids can't be made fun of for dressing different. Life doesn't work that way, because things are never equal.

Even though he's in sixth grade, Rodrigo Luis has the body of a third grader who had a diet of only leaves and water. He talks fast and is always up to no good, which is something, considering I'm the one saying it. And he has impulse control issues. But I tell you what, his pants have a crisp crease in them and his red shirt doesn't even have a hint of fade to its color. When he stands, he turns his collar up, dismissing the world.

The air leaves the room as they file in and sit next to me. It's like we're afraid to speak, so we exchange guilty glances. I can't help but picture us as being in a police lineup. The Mrs. Fitzgerald we were used to would have just popped down to our class and met us on our turf if she had something to say. But this time she summoned us to her office. She bridges her fingers in front of her face and waits, like a per-turbed cat about to pounce on all the unsuspecting mice lured to her cave.

Mrs. Horner waddles into the room with the walk of someone whose joints ache. She's the lead facil-itator of the special education class. Not teachers, facilitators. This is typical of how me and my friends are singled out. Believe me, I never felt special. Or facilitated. Her egg-shaped body totters back and forth as she makes her way to a seat. She runs her clawlike hand through her white-edged black hair.

Mr. Blackmon trails all of them and shuts the door behind him. Short, barely taller than me, his skin the shade of sunbaked cinnamon—only a shade darker than mine—he also has that quiet swagger. A young dude with smooth pretty-boy looks, black-framed glasses perched on his nose just like he's stepping out of a "smart guys on campus" fashion shoot. But his head is tiny, like a peanut I want to flick across the room. Also one of the special education facilitators, Mr. Blackmon's duties include escorting special education students to the common classes we share with the "regular" (since they're not "special") students: recess, lunch, gym, art, and music.

Mrs. Horner and Mr. Blackmon retreat to the back wall, as far from Mrs. Fitzgerald as possible, letting us know that whatever was about to go down, we were on our own. It's the first time I actually get nervous about this meeting. If our teachers are uncomfortable enough to want to stay out of collateral-damage range, something was definitely up.

Mr. Blackmon hesitates a second while he studies my face. Knowing when I am being scanned for any sign of trouble, I turn my smile up to eleven. Everyone should have their go-to faces for special occasions. My "I'm being charming" face. Or my "who me?" face I break out when the maximum appearance of innocence is needed. My moms says

I have a resting "up to something" face, so it rarely matters what face I put on, especially my "who me?" one. Mr. Blackmon seems more skeptical of me than ever.

"Good morning, class," says Mrs. Fitzgerald.

"Good morning, Mrs. Fitzgerald," we say in unison.

"We have a serious problem and I thought it was important that we discuss it." Mrs. Fitzgerald studies each of our faces with something barely softer than a glare.

No one dares roll his eyes. No one dares cross his arms. No one dares chance a grin. Not even the boldest among us—and I do mean Nehemiah—feels safe enough to do anything more than sit there, hands in laps, paying wide-eyed attention.

"Yesterday, next door at Northwestway Park, some young people found something. Does anyone know what?" Mrs. Fitzgerald walks around her desk like a lawyer in a courtroom giving an opening statement. (Moms has a thing for crime shows.)

Mrs. Fitzgerald's words hang in the air. All we

can do is shake our heads, but without too much enthusiasm. It was like the group of us inched across a frozen lake, not knowing if or when we'd find a thin spot in the ice and go crashing through.

"A grocery bag wadded into a ball. It was heavy so they unwrapped it." Mrs. Fitzgerald pauses, probably for effect. She knows how to put on a show and right now she has all our silent attention. "Inside was a gun."

"Ooh," everyone says.

Well, almost everyone. I lean back in my seat and cross my arms. I've seen this movie play out many times before. Something goes missing? Must be one of us. Something gets broken? Must be one of us. I know where this story is headed because the last time they "investigated" something, Twon wound up blamed anyway and suspended. And he wasn't even around.

"Being responsible and cautious, they called over a couple of our custodians who were doing their jobs. Taking care of the building and keeping Persons clean and secure. We know that the park is a popular hangout for all of you. So I wanted to impress on you that this is a very grave matter." When Mrs. Fitzgerald is on a roll, she can give the best preacher a run for their money. "We turned the gun over to the police. This was too close to our school. We strive to maintain a safe environment here at Persons. We want you to be safe. We want our staff to be safe. We want our visitors to be safe. There isn't any reason to bring a weapon near this building. Not to impress anyone. Not to scare any-one. Not to threaten anyone. It won't be tolerated."

After a few heartbeats, I speak up. "And you think one of us brought it."

Everyone else stares at me with their mouths hanging open, gawking like I'd grown a third arm out of my back.

"When something goes wrong, you just bring in the usual suspects," I finish.

They turn their attention slowly back to Mrs. Fitzgerald and hold their breath, waiting to see just how much of my head she was about to shred.

"It's not like that, Thelonius. What is it we say?

We STEP our problems: *S*ay the problem, *T*hink of solutions, *E*xplore consequences, *P*ick the best solutions. I wanted to impress on each and every one of our students just how seriously we are going to treat it. We're going to conduct a full and thorough investigation. We're going to be talking to a lot of students."

Starting with us. I open my mouth to begin saying it, but the words catch in my throat. Like when you're about to say something smart in church after getting away with one comment but you know the next might get you snatched into next week. I had used up all the attitude I could muster in Mrs. Fitzgerald's presence and chose to keep my thoughts to myself. Besides, they can talk all they want about doing an investigation, but they're not going to get too much truth out of us. Lying to adults is how we breathe.

"But now that you've brought it up," she continues, as if reading my mind, "I have been reconsidering how the special education room operates. Trouble does seem to follow you. Mr. Caldwell over there is on strike two and his third would have him automatically expelled. And I'm pretty sure there are some pitches thrown that the facilitators haven't bothered counting."

Nehemiah shrinks in his seat, but side-eyes me as if I put him on blast.

"We're having all our teachers talk to their classes today. I wanted to personally inform some of the students. I will be sending a letter home with each of you apprising your parents of the situation. Messages will go out to their phones and emails, too, so you might as well give the letter to them. We'll be doing a full school assembly at the end of the week. Anything we learn from our investigation we'll share then. But everyone is on notice." Mrs. Fitzgerald eases back in her chair. The air squishes out of it with a gentle sigh.

"Let me make this perfectly clear, gentlemen: if someone comes forward by the end of the week, I will consider a lenient punishment. But if I find out someone in this class is the culprit and others are helping to cover it up, this entire class will be transferred to the Banesford Accelerated Academy."

There is a collective gasp. Banesford Accelerated Academy is the boogeyman teachers threaten us kids with. A charter school alternative to juvenile detention, Banesford focuses on kids who have serious discipline problems at their respective schools. In other words, it is a whole school made up of all the other kids schools gave up on. Rumors spread about how strict they are there. How kids get detention for not having their pencils sharpened. How students are only allowed to talk during recess and for five minutes at lunch.

I can only imagine how Moms is going to react to all this. The bottom falls out of my stomach.

I've been accused of a lot of things, some worse than others, but this here? Hiding a gun near the school? This is beyond me. It's criminal. It's hard enough to go to school with the idea that a shooting could happen. Grown folks only whisper about it because it terrifies them and that fear's like a virus they know is easy to pass on so they try to vaccinate us. But no matter how hard they avoid bringing it up, we hear about it. On TV. On the radio. On the internet. And we try not to think about it, like we do all the other big things that are out of our control.

Then I get accused of this.

That crosses a line. That's an attack on me, who I am at my core. I may do some knucklehead stuff, but accusing me of that leaves a stain on a person. They're trying to do me dirty.

The more I think about it, the more heated I get.

I understand that folks have a job to do and all, and things would be different if I'd actually done something. I have done plenty I could be busted on. But I can't stand being blamed for stuff I didn't do. Which happens all the time. I hate living under a cloud of constantly being accused. It just gets so frustrating, all I can do is act out. I guess if I've got impulse control issues, I just can't help myself. I wish I had a distraction, like planning my next move with my boys, but I can't because our schedules have separated us for our noncore classes, so I need a target to vent my frustration on.

Luckily we have that same sub for World Music today.

The substitute music teacher has the stink of being an easy mark all over him. His pin-striped black suit over a red vest makes him look like he is dressed to impress at a board meeting. A newbie sub, he reads and rereads the lesson plan, studying it as if trying to commit Scripture to memory. The man has probably never even been to a music session in his life, yet here he staggers about, playing at being a music teacher for the day. Walking to the front of the class, he hesitates with the dry erase marker at the whiteboard as if struggling to remember how to spell his own name. As far as I am concerned, he's a new chew toy whose name I wouldn't bother remembering.

Rows of chairs arranged in a semicircle face the raised stage. The students begin to whisper, low at first, one eye kept on the sub to see what noise level would draw his attention and cause him to try to quiet us.

"What goes around the world but stays in a corner?" Squinting as if under a spotlight, and sweating in the same way, the sub wears a desperate grin. "A stamp."

The class groans. A corny joke to get on our good side? That's a straight-up rookie move. This is almost too painful to watch.

Suddenly I appreciate how Mr. Blackmon is the opposite of the sub. Relaxed and sure of himself, he's an old hand at the teaching game despite being much younger. Tapping me on the shoulder and nodding toward the substitute teacher, Mr. Blackmon quietly encourages me to pay attention. *This is corny*, I want to say, but I can almost hear him respond with *It's important to respect whoever the teacher is*. He has a series of "structure isn't your enemy" speeches.

A door across the hallway slams so hard it rattles the one to the music room. Shouting fills the hall, prompting all heads to turn toward the disturbance. I recognize the raised voice of my dude Nehemiah. I'm not the only one acting out due to frustration, though a solid draft of air would be enough to send him off wilding. A smile creeps across my face. The timing couldn't be have been more perfect if we had planned it.

Mr. Blackmon leans over to me. "I have to go see about that."

"You know it's just Nehemiah popping off." I keep my attention on the sub, not daring Mr. Blackmon to read anything on my face.

"I'll just be gone a minute. Behave." He overpronounces each syllable of *behave* like it was a foreign word to me.

"I promise, Mr. Blackmon, I'll just sit here." A ring of innocence fills my voice so thick it comes out almost singsongy. I flash two fingers in a peace sign. "Deuces."

The door barely closes behind Mr. Blackmon before I turn my attention back to the class. I run my tongue over my lips. People are easy marks for me. Underneath their fancy suits or school uniforms, they are all the same. Everyone has their weak spots. You just have to know how to push them.

Everyone has a gift. My gift is words. I know how to make up a story.

I duck down in my seat and bring my sheet music up to my face. I pretend to study it, but actually it makes for a good shield. With the sub unable to see my lips move, I turn to my left. "Hey, my guy."

"What's up?" Jaron Andemichael wears the

same red short-sleeved polo shirt and navy blue pants the other boys do. However, Jaron hit a growth spurt after his mother bought his school clothes for the year. His shirt barely covers his belly, riding up whenever he moves. He's a big dude and usually people assume he has a temper. Don't get me wrong, my dude could throw with the best of them when riled up, but most people don't see him. He rarely meets anyone's eyes for fear of them locking on to him and picking on him about his weight. And the more he gets picked on, the more he eats, so he walks the halls like a big, nervous squirrel.

"I ain't trying to meddle in your business. I'm a live-and-let-live sort of dude. But I hear things. If it's none of my business, just let me know." I press my hand to my chest to emphasize that I'm more than willing to back off and mind my own.

"What'd you hear?" Jaron suddenly can't get comfortable in his chair. He studies his classmates, his eyes accusing each of them.

"You see that light-skinned dude with the beaver teeth and goofy glasses? I heard him talking about you. About how you never met a cheeseburger you didn't like."

"He said that?" Jaron sits up straighter, anger slowly filling his eyes. Like I say, everyone has their snapping point. Everyone has that limit where they grow tired of what people assume or say about them. When they can't take any more and just want to put the world on notice to leave them alone.

"Word is bond. He says you have to go to a special Goodwill to get your shirts 'cause no one stocks sizes with that many *X*'s in them. And the stuff he says about your momma . . ."

"What'd he say about my momma?" Jaron balls up his sheet music in his meaty fists.

What was the point of trying to be better when other folks always believed the worst about you? Sometimes you just want to give in and be what they believe you are.

"I don't know the woman, so I'm not making any judgments, but he was saying how she don't cook. She just shovels food into a trough, then rings a bell to have you come eat."

"That . . ." Jaron springs up and dashes across the room.

The sound of a chair scraping the floor causes the sub to pause mid-writing on the whiteboard the list of classwork to be completed today and turn around. The sight of Jaron charging toward another student with murderous intent freezes him. While the sub gathers himself to figure out what to do next, I turn to my right.

With a sly glance, I study the boy. Sweat-streaked dirt rings his shirt collar. Something greasy smears his wrinkled pants. His shoes flop with each step as the sole separates from the rest of it. "Hey, my dude."

"My name's RaShawn. Hold up, man, I want to see this." RaShawn Lothery, like I didn't already know his name, crouches half out of his chair in order to sneak a peek.

The sub wraps his arms around Jaron, but in a tentative way, not wanting to injure him. Or just scared of being sued later. But Jaron is a beefy kid, much larger and harder to get ahold of, especially when he's all worked up.

"That's cool. I probably ought to stay out of what folks are saying about you anyway." I lean back in my chair with a cool disinterest.

RaShawn keeps one eye on the fight, but the other returns to me. "What'd you say?"

"Just that some folks were talking crazy about you."

"Who? What'd they say?" RaShawn climbs down from the chair like a slowly deflating balloon.

I angle my head toward a kid cheering on the chaos from his seat of Jaron acting buck wild. The sub accidentally catches an elbow to the side of his face when he steps in front of Jaron, who was attempting to throw punches. "Little man over there."

"Yeah, he got a mouth on him," RaShawn says with a sneer.

"Sure do. Going on about how poor you are. Talking about how you have to wear your clothes three, four days in a row because you can't afford to do laundry." I lace my hands behind my head. Winding people up as much as I'm wound up seems about right.

"He got some nerve, him and his raggedy, country behind."

"That's what *I'm* saying. He all up in your Kool-Aid, putting your business on blast. And the stuff he says about your momma . . ." I press my left hand to my chest and wave my right as if the news was too much and I can't bear to go on.

RaShawn leans forward. "What'd he say about my momma?"

"I don't know the woman, so I'm not making any judgments, but he was saying that she's out every night, you know . . ."

RaShawn erupts with a stream of profanity so loud everyone in the classroom stops where they are. The target of his sudden wrath barely has time to angle toward him in his chair before RaShawn leaps. He tackles the boy and the pair tumble onto the raised platform in front of the class. They wrestle along the carpeted area. The cymbals clang as RaShawn and the other boy roll into them. The bass drum pounds an irregular rhythm as they thrash about.

Still wrapped in the sub's bear hug, Jaron continues to swing his arms. He wrenches free of the teacher. Jaron jumps on the man's back when he steps between them as he attempts to grab the boy.

"Fight! Fight! Fight!" the class chants.

Mr. Blackmon opens the door. Despite RaShawn and one boy knocking over music stands and the sub separating Jaron from another boy, Mr. Blackmon walks straight to me. "What's going on here, Thelonius?" he asks, unfazed by the classroom bedlam.

"Nothing, Mr. Blackmon." I pretend to be studying my sheet music as if trying to concentrate despite the chaos. "I'm trying to do my work, but it's hard with all the distractions. The sub don't know how to keep control of his class."

"I suppose you had nothing to do with it?" Mr. Blackmon sighs with disappointment.

"Nothing at all. I'm hurt that you could think such a thing." I catch myself as my hand moves to my chest to protest my innocence. That kind of theatricality would be insulting to both of us.

"Hey!" Mr. Blackmon shouts.

Like a spell suddenly being broken, all the fighting stops. Mr. Blackmon hooks my arm and escorts me from the classroom, allowing the substitute to regain control. I chance one last look at the scene before the door closes behind me. The overturned instruments, Jaron and RaShawn hyped up. The kind of handiwork I'd normally be kind of pleased with, but it feels a little hollow today. It's too much a picture of how I feel: angry, amped up to fight, and leaving a mess that only really hurts the people around me.

Mr. Blackmon's disappointed sigh rings in my ears.

I can't move through the halls without feeling
the weight of everyone's eyes on me, like invisible
fingers pointing. I'm used to people feeling some sort
of way about me, but this is different. More like they
might be afraid. Mrs. Horner watches me with suspicion from the second Mr. Blackmon opens the door.

Mrs. Horner sees us and her instinct is to swat
us. I call it the Spider Syndrome: when people see
a spider, their eyes light up and their hearts race
because they're scared. They're so panicked they
forget the thing that's terrifying them is often, like,
one hundred times smaller than they are. All they

know is all the bad stories they hear about them, how deadly a bite from one of them can be even though that only applies to a small fraction of them. Spiders look strange to them, different and ugly. Their ways confuse and alarm people like them— the way they skitter across a room, lower themselves unexpectedly on a strand, how they leave messy webs wherever they go. So when a person sees one, they're conditioned to smash it. It's easy to believe bad stories and let them color how you see things.

Shaking his head, Mr. Blackmon sips from the bottle of water he always carries around with him. I slow walk over to the sink in the back of the Special Ed room to primp in front of the mirror over it. I slant my head several ways to make sure each strand of my thick coils of braids is in place. Not that I'm vain or anything, I'm just still undecided about how they look on me. My aunt laced a red cord into each braid. Now that I'm coming down from showing out, I'm growing anxious at the thought of having to confront Moms and explain the latest thing I have been all but accused of doing. Me acting up is one thing. She isn't going to sweat the small stuff. Me accused of a felony or whatever, that's going to take Moms to a new level.

Mr. Blackmon coughs to draw my attention, and points toward my seat. With his arms crossed, he hovers about my desk. And he sighs all dramatic-like.

"Why you so mad, Mr. Blackmon?" Imitating the tone he usually takes with me, I pat him on the shoulder as I move toward my seat.

"I thought we were making some progress with your . . . tendencies. I'm just disappointed."

"Don't be so hard on yourself." I attempt to sound as sympathetic as possible. "Keep your head up. You're doing fine."

I smile. When I smile, most folks can't help but be less mad at me. It's another gift.

"Just have a seat." Mr. Blackmon takes another quick swig of the bottled water. He closes the lid up, letting the clear gray container dangle off his finger by a single black loop. I imagine him as a gunslinger in the old West, twirling the bottle around his finger before holstering it. I have a theory that he conveniently drinks whenever he's about to break character and smile. He's all about maintaining his firm but fair image.

Though Twon, Rodrigo, and Pierce weren't in their normal classes, the Special Ed room is unusually quiet. Until Nehemiah makes his entrance. He stops at the threshold and jumps to see if he can touch the upper trim. His slap echoes loudly, drawing all attention to him, so he slowly struts into the room. Mrs. Horner is on him like a hawk, waiting for him to slip up. That boy loves to clown. He meanders by the mirror, brushing the slight waves in his hair. No matter how much time he spends in front of the mirror, he somehow never catches the thin crusty film that always frames his mouth.

A couch and television area separate the desks from the six computers that line the back wall. They face the only windows in the room. After collecting my to-do list from Mrs. Horner, I speed through the day's math assignment. The material's so easy it's almost insulting, not that I'm complaining. My fingers dance along the keyboard like a spider hyped up on Mountain Dew. Through the blinds, we have a view of the parking lot and the playground. Staring out the window and slipping the computer's headphones on, I lose myself in my thoughts. Finally I can breathe again and concentrate clearly.

I can't believe someone brought a gun to the park. Well, I guess I can. It's close enough to the school that if they needed it, they only had to jog a little bit from the playground to get it. No matter where you go, there's always someone bigger, stronger, meaner than you and they have no problem reminding you who's the rabbit and who's the hyena. Sometimes you just get sick of being the rabbit all the time. Some folks cope by puffing up like they're a hyena or at least threatening enough to make the hyena move on. After all, most hyenas have water in their veins and are just looking for the easiest prey.

Nehemiah strides toward the computer area. He slows and we clap hands, interlock our index fingers, and spin our hands to lock thumbs. We form gun barrels with our fingers, shoot them to each side and snap our fingers. That's our special handshake. Just for us.

"You need some lotion." No one else dares mention it because he's so quick to anger. Just about anything sets him off, zero to Hulk in 3.4 seconds. Everyone tiptoes around him, scared. Everyone except me.

"Settle down, friends." Mrs. Horner can save that "friends" nonsense. The word always sounds phony in her mouth, like she's one of those politicians who says things that makes sense to some people but not others. But we all know what they're really about.

Nehemiah draws up a seat quietly next to me and flicks on the computer. Like I said, everyone has a gift. Here's the thing about Nehemiah: he's a wizard with a computer. The hacking of the library computers so I could play online poker? That was him. Because she doesn't see him, I don't think Mrs. Horner has a clue about how good he is. She's convinced he's cheating somehow on his assignments. Don't get me wrong, he is, but he's breaking the code of the education software through some back door he discovered in the program (I don't know what he's going on about most times with this computer code stuff). The thing is that it all sounds much harder than if he just did the math work itself, so he should probably get the A anyway.

Nehemiah adjusts the headphones so that the ear closest to me remains uncovered. He slumps toward me and begins in a conspiratorial whisper, "Can you believe someone brought a gun around here?"

"The only thing I can't believe is that this is the first time it's happened." I focus on my screen, not betraying our conversation more than I have to. "Man, Mrs. Fitzgerald don't play. She is straight-up gangsta."

"She as gangsta as *My Little Pony*." No one impresses Nehemiah, not that he'd ever let on if they did. "Still, I wish we could've seen it."

"Like you've never seen a gun before." I side-eye him.

"It's different."

"Because it's at school?"

"Yeah."

I suspect that conversations like this are happening all over the building at this moment. The idea of being called to the principal's office over it still rubs me wrong. No matter what words came out of her mouth, I know what Mrs. Fitzgerald really means: the Special Ed class is on notice, and as soon as enough evidence is collected, someone, or someones, was going to be expelled and sent to Banesford.

"Nehemiah, can I ask you something?"

"Go ahead."

I lean forward and stare him directly in his eyes. "Was it you?"

"How you going to ask me that, T?" Nehemiah springs up, knocking his chair over onto the carpet.

Mrs. Horner glances up from her desk. "Is there a problem back there?"

"No, Mrs. Horner." My eyes beg for Nehemiah to have a seat. I can't afford for him to pop off all "Hulk smash!" style right now. Too much is at stake.

"Pick up the chair and finish your work," Mrs. Horner says.

"Come on. We got this, okay?" I whisper. "It's all good."

"So why'd you come at me like that?" Nehemiah

barely manages a whisper. His whole body shakes, drawing Mr. Blackmon's attention. If he comes over with one of his hand-on-the-shoulder moves, Nehemiah would fully erupt and they'd spend the next half hour chasing him through the halls.

"You always talking about the rough stuff your brothers get into. Almost bragging."

"'Cause their foolishness is funny. But I ain't them."

"Look, you know what all the teachers are thinking: we all guilty. One of us. All of us." I throw my hands up. "I don't know, all this stuff plays in our heads after a while. . . . I had to ask."

With those words, my anger toward Mrs. Horner softens. But only a little. I'm more ashamed of myself. Nehemiah is like the rest of us, going through life accused all the time. This one day when she came back to the room to find her coffee cup broken, Mrs. Horner keyed in on Nehemiah. Rode him ragged. Questioned him, talked about his lack of home training, all in front of the class. Soon after, the janitor came in and apologized for knocking it over. No "I'm sorry" crossed her lips in Nehemiah's direction, only a "you didn't do it this time" sneer. I'm pretty sure life isn't supposed to be lived so on the defensive. My attention bounces from him to my screen. "I take that back. I shouldn't have asked."

"I didn't ask *you*," Nehemiah emphasizes.

"I know."

Somewhat mollified, Nehemiah relaxes a little. "Well, for the record, your honor, I didn't have anything to do with that gun."

I crack half a smile at him. "Once I thought about it, if you had brought it to the park, your crazy self would have run up and down the basketball courts, waving it around until you got tackled."

Maybe not waving it around. A brother's got to be discreet. It's all about the threat. Nehemiah straightens with sudden pride. "What's the point of carrying it if no one knows you got it."

"Yeah . . ." I drift off. In the distance, sixth graders run up and down the playground basketball court, little more than blobs of color scurrying about in the throes of recess. They all look so young, but old enough to all be potential suspects. Or victims. This feels so . . . big. I don't want to see any of them hurt. If I can help find any information to keep them safe . . .

"Everyone come into community circle." Mrs. Horner's announcement interrupts my thoughts. "I have something I want to talk about."

She reminds me of the old-school principal before Mrs. Fitzgerald. Mrs. Horner no longer cared. Most of the time she just sits at her desk, playing on her phone. She only acts busy if Mrs. Fitzgerald comes by or if one of us misbehaves enough (or too loudly for her to concentrate on scrolling through Facebook or whatever). Even then, she's more annoyed at having to deal with us than wanting to teach us. The computer programs give us our assignments, Mr. Blackmon manages us, leaving her like a football coach playing out the clock at the end of a game.

Actually, school is one big game and there is an unspoken contract between teacher and student. Teachers, facilitators, and administrators have their jobs: telling us what to do. Go here, go there, do this, do that. No, this way. Start over and do it again. And again. And again. Now we students have our own job, too: make their jobs as hard to do as possible.

As if the simple effort to push ourselves up from our chairs is too much for us, we start grumbling as soon as Mrs. Horner stops talking. I roll my eyes for good measure. Nehemiah slams his pencil into his desk, pretending that her request somehow interrupted the flow of the work he had no intention of doing. He laps the room, passing our "Reward Store," which has all sorts of treats for good behavior (so, pretty much the only time he ever gets near it), stopping for a drink of water at the sink, making quite the production of his protest march before heading toward the gathering.

Twon seems a little slow, but he has a way about him. I have a theory that people get blessed with certain traits, but there is only so much heart to go around. People can't handle being both sweet and extra-gifted. So some folks, like me, double dipped for talents, charm, and good looks. I'm just saying. People like Twon received extra heart. It's all about priorities of who you wanted to be. This is just a working theory.

Rodrigo raises his index finger to ask for one minute. The second Mrs. Horner and Mr. Blackmon turn away, he flips off the rest of the class. He can't help himself.

"Come on, Pierce," Twon says to the last kid remaining in his seat. "Mrs. Horner wants us all in community circle."

"It's okay. Leave Pierce alone," Mrs. Horner says. "He's doing his work."

"Yeah, plus he has that creepy stare. I don't need to deal with that before lunch," Rodrigo whispers.

Pierce Lyons is in sixth grade, but is so small for his size he looks like he could've been in third. With his blond hair trimmed down to military length, a thick cloud of freckles dots each cheek. His regular teacher even leaves him in here to eat his lunch at a desk. Like Nehemiah, he violates the school uniform policy with regularity. Unlike Nehemiah, he wears a sweater vest and necktie, which make him look like he wandered in from some upscale private academy.

The colors almost match the Persons Crossing Public Academy colors, so Mrs. Horner lets it slide.

Then again, if there's a student Mrs. Horner tends to favor, it's Pierce. She holds out hope for him, I guess. We aren't dumb. We know if his skin was darker, he'd be deemed as much a lost cause as the rest of us. It's the other reason we tune her out. There's something to be said for self-preservation.

The vaulted ceilings hide recessed fluorescent lights that call attention to the row of student names: Thelonius, Nehemiah, Twon, Rodrigo, Pierce, Brionna. Centered between them is a quote: "In a world where you can be anything . . . *be yourself*!" The carpet of the Special Ed room matches the rest of the school with its pink-against-maroon pattern woven into it. The wall with the whiteboard fixed to it is a faded red. This is the only room in the school with anything close to pink in it. Some genius convinced someone gullible along the way that the color scheme would be soothing. Burgundy cubbies hold our coats, backpacks, and lunch boxes along the wall farthest from the door. Cabinets hang over a sink on the side where the time-out closet is. Its door dangles open, like an expectant mouth eager to devour the next kid that acts out. That's why most kids called it the "Scream Room" instead.

"Raise your hands if you've come back to the class and found your stuff messed with or stolen." Mrs. Horner starts her morning lecture she calls community circle. Community circle was supposed to be about sharing frustrations and working through our feelings. I swear teachers have nothing better to do than come up with new ways for us to think about our feelings. Feelings we got. Communicating our feelings we got. When Nehemiah takes off his shirt and screams at people, even the dullest detective in the world can pick up on his feelings. Most days Mrs. Horner simmers, just as frustrated as us, except she works through her feelings by punishing us. We just have to take it . . . while thinking about our feelings.

Just about every hand shoots up in answer to her question. Now, my things have never been even remotely disrespected. The problem is that I don't want to be the lone hand unraised. That would look funny. Maybe I'm too suspicious, but I wonder if part of the game Mrs. Horner plays at involves pitting one of us against the others, and letting peer pressure do its thing. My hand shoots up.

"That's what I thought. We go out of our way to make sure you have all the school supplies you need to do your work. These things are here for you to use, not abuse." Mrs. Horner paces back and forth, forcing all eyes to be on her, a trick she picked up from Mrs. Fitzgerald. She talks slow and soft, forcing us to lean in to hear her. "Mr. Blackmon went out of his way, spent his own money, to get you all name tags with the multiplication tables on them."

I pay attention to Mr. Blackmon during Mrs. Horner's rants. That dude is hilarious without saying a word. He sits against one of the front desks but right behind us like he was one of the boys. Half the time she treats him like that, too. A pained expression crosses his face, like he's eaten three-day-old raw fish, whenever she talks like they're on the same team. He sips from his water bottle.

"In one week, twenty pencils. Gone. Twenty pens.

Gone. It'd be different if you were doing enough work to use them up, but you're obviously not."

Mr. Blackmon winces again. He brings the bottle to his mouth, turns it up with disappointment on his face, and lifts it closer for further inspection. It's empty.

"Why you always be accusing us?" Nehemiah jerks his shoulders forward out of reflex, used to brushing off any attempt to touch him.

"*Cuz you always be doin' stuff.*" Mrs. Horner never fails to sound condescending whenever she tries to talk to us using our words.

Mr. Blackmon pinches the bridge of his nose and shakes his head.

"I've divided up the rest of our materials. Every supply you need is in the pencil supply box in your desks." Mrs. Horner steps back and sweeps her arm by the reorganized supplies like she's a game show hostess.

"You went into our desks?" Nehemiah sucks his teeth in disgust and jumps up to check his things. "That's some bull."

Mrs. Horner pauses to let Nehemiah settle down.

When she realizes he's determined not to pay any further attention, she continues a little louder to cover his muttering. "When things go missing, it ruins the fun for everyone and that's not fair. I expect this to be a nonissue from now on. Give me two claps if you understand what I'm saying."

Two unenthusiastic claps, not quite in unison, follow. Of course this is what she cares about: missing supplies. Not a mention about the gun. I guess she's like them police who solve crime by fixing broken lampposts. You go ahead and fix that broken window while I'm shot up on the corner.

Checking the time, 10:50 a.m., I have my Humanities homework to do. With a stroll so lazy Nehemiah would have been proud of it—if he wasn't so caught up in making sure all his things were in the mess he called a desk—I headed toward mine. Out the corner of my eye, I watch Mr. Blackmon approach. It's like he times himself to interrupt my flow.

"Thelonius, can I talk with you for a second?" Mr. Blackmon's water bottle still drips from being refilled. He drags a chair from the nearest desk over to me.

"Sure, Mr. Blackmon. What you need?" I ease back in my seat and strike my the-doctor-is-in pose.

I have to admit, Mr. Blackmon isn't like the other folks who pass through Special Ed. Most folks fall into one of two camps: the burnouts, like Mrs. Horner, who came in day after day to collect their checks and whatever else it was old teachers do when they lose their joy; or the do-gooders, who try a bit too hard to relate to us but are mostly in here to study us so they can "change the system." They ask a lot of questions, write a lot of papers, and pat themselves on their backs a lot for doing . . . something. Mr. Blackmon actually seems to care, though that doesn't make him above being messed with.

"What do you think about what Mrs. Horner just said?" he asks.

"I agree with Nehemiah. She's always accusing us. I guess it's going to be that kind of day."

"I get that. That part's on her. What about the part that's on you?" Mr. Blackmon cocks his head. A bit of sympathy drips from his tone, but that head angle means he wants to drill into me for a while.

"What do you mean?"

"You don't think that somewhere along the line, in your history, you may have done things that have earned you . . . a bit of a reputation?"

Pausing for a second, I sift through my words carefully. There is a trap in his question somewhere, I am pretty sure of it. "What are you getting at?"

"First Mrs. Fitzgerald has her talk with us. Then Mrs. Horner has her talk with us. I was just wondering how you were taking it all," he says without accusation.

Shifting in my seat, I turn away from him. This dude's always trying to get in my feels. I'm no saint, but I'm no felon either. That's the way it goes, though: they get used to blaming you for little stuff and it's easy for them to put the heavy stuff on you, too. This here has some serious weight to it and I know I'm not the one to carry it. Whoever it is will be in a world of trouble we ain't ready for, though. I half mutter something along those lines and stop because it felt too . . . real.

"What was that?" Mr. Blackmon asks.

"What I meant to say was that it don't seem right for her to just blame us for stuff. But that's the way it always goes, I guess."

Mr. Blackmon leans back like he needs a moment to gather his thoughts. He glances up. Right above us, signs dangle along the wall:

EMPATHY

Is feeling or understanding what
someone else is feeling.
Compassion is empathy in action.

RESPECT ONE ANOTHER

- use manners
- be a good sport
- be helpful
- follow directions
- USE EMPATHY!

When I read them, the signs seem like another attempt at brainwashing from the teachers. That's the thing—I have to constantly be on guard against all the messages they want to program into us. Again, I could almost hear Mr. Blackmon's voice say how my *hypervigilance and paranoia are an unnecessary defense mechanism.* But of course he has to say that; the signs were his idea.

"What are you thinking about doing with your life?" Mr. Blackmon asks.

Like I said, he's always about the feels. "I don't know. If I make it to next week, maybe I'll give it some thought."

"You're telling me that a young man of the world, like yourself, as bright as you are, hasn't thought at all about any future plans?"

"Maybe I'll be a drug dealer. Is that what you want to hear? That's all anyone expects of me anyway." Raising my voice a little, I nod toward Mrs. Horner.

"That's not true, Thelonius. I expect great things from you." Mr. Blackmon rests a hand on my shoulder. He can be so corny sometimes.

"Mr. Blackmon, you married?"

"Yeah, nine years. To my high school sweetheart as a matter of fact."

"Who does that? You straight-up got no game." I

hunch over a bit more in my seat to pounce on this revelation. And convenient change of topic. "Any kids?"

"Two, a five- and a six-year-old. Why?"

"Just trying to figure out if you're missing anything at home. The way you always coming over here to talk, I figured you were lonely or something. Are you lonely, Mr. Blackmon?" I clap my hand on Mr. Blackmon's shoulder. I keep my face as solemn as I can for as long as I can before a smile cracks through.

Mr. Blackmon swallows another gulp of water.

The door swings open, and Brionna Davidson saunters in. A sixth grader with a thick head of serpentine braids, each of which has three white beads dangling from the tips, she breezes in and out of class at will. She and her teachers came to a bit of an informal agreement: whenever she began to get too worked up, too anxious or "full of energy" as she put it, they let her walk down to the Special Ed room to take a break. Mrs. Horner supervises the administration of her meds here rather than at the nurse's office.

"You need your pills, honey?" Mrs. Horner asks. She's also softer with girls.

"Yeah." Brionna hops up on her desk to have a seat while she waits.

"Can I use the restroom?" Nehemiah always tries to work Mrs. Horner when she seems distracted. The problem is that she is never so distracted that she doesn't see him coming.

"Have you earned any time by doing your work?" she asks.

"Dang." Nehemiah breaks the word, pronouncing it like it has two syllables. He crumples up a sheet of paper and throws it at her desk. Mrs. Horner reaches for the blue stack of papers, reflection forms to be filled out whenever a student misbehaves. A form means automatic after-school detention. Nehemiah stops himself, finds the piece of paper, and smooths it out for her approval.

"Fine. I don't want to hear your fussing." Taking a casual survey of his work, she sets the blue sheet down and fills out a hall pass instead.

Nehemiah trots toward the door but stops at my desk. Flexing his thin arms and balling his hands into fists, he lunges his chest forward. I duck backward.

"You flinched." Nehemiah punches me twice.

"This is a stupid game. Of course I flinched. You ain't exactly the most in-control dude I know. You might swing and hit me by accident."

"Whatever." Nehemiah squints like he just noticed me for the first time. "What's up? You got your scheming face on."

"If nothing else, we need to figure out who brought that gun to school before this whole situation finds a way to fall on us."

"What are we going to do? You got a plan?" Nehemiah glances toward Mrs. Horner before dropping to a knee pretending to tie his shoelace.

"Not sure yet. I'm just at the thinking stage. First up, though, I need to talk to Moms before she hears Mrs. Fitzgerald's message."

4

The bus driver snails through the streets, never in any particular hurry.

First the bus lurches out of the school parking lot, belching black smoke, grumbling along the side street that winds from Persons Crossing Public Academy to the main road. Traffic backs up behind it. Cars are too scared to dart around it because this stretch of road is a well-known speed trap. With each stop, I recalculate what story to give Moms that might spare my life.

The gray road gives way to rows of trees that tick by with the rumble of the bus as my soundtrack.

I picture Moms stomping around my room like Godzilla, her yelling worse than any radioactive breath. The rows of trees give way to the houses of our addition. Though traveling the same route the bus always takes, it seems like the bus driver, Mrs. McGhee, has gone out of her way to snake through the neighborhood. She yields to the buses from other schools, which crisscross the subdivision. She stops at every house. She brakes to allow plenty of time for squirrels to scamper in front. What should be a five-minute trek adds several years to my life while I sweat what I'm going to tell Moms.

Our house sits on a blind curve. Traffic can't see through the thick stand of trees that guards the edge of our property. It doesn't matter how many signs we plant or how often Moms yells at them, kids dash across the road like they can't be hit. I find myself leaning to the side as if somehow I could then see around the final bend of my street. Moms drives a blue Prizm, a 1992 edition. She doesn't care that the paint is peeling from the hood. The car runs well and is paid off. I pray long and hard that when we find our way around the curve that her car won't be parked in the driveway like some predatory bird waiting to swoop down and snatch me up whole. On the other hand, if I do see it, I at least have a few moments to mentally brace myself for Hurricane Moms.

I have a theory that the best way to control a story is to be the one telling it. It's like a truth inoculation. You know, like when you go to the doctor to get immunized, they give you a shot that's a little bit of the thing they're trying to protect you against? A little bit of it triggers your body to protect itself. In this case, I need to give Moms a careful amount of the truth to protect her against the full truth. So actually this is for her own good.

When we follow the bend, it isn't the car in the driveway that makes me both sigh and send my heart tumbling into my stomach. It's the sight of my mother squaring off against a teenage girl. While a growing crowd of neighborhood kids surrounds them.

"Oh snap." Nehemiah prepares to join me at my

stop. He rarely rides all the way to his home since no one would be there, especially this soon after school. "Moms is about to go off."

I scramble to collect my stuff and slink off the bus.

"Oooo," the twins say at the same time. Tafrica Simone and Wisdom Monet aren't related and don't look like each other. Tafrica has skin the color of rich sepia, her hair styled into a nest of thick braids. Wisdom, short for Wisdom-Madonna, has the complexion of milk with a dab of butter in it. She has long blond hair woven into two braids and a face that's perfect with her glasses. The two all but hold hands wherever they go, a continuous fountain of gossip.

"Who's that with your mom?" Wisdom blocks me, ignoring how anxious I am to get off at my stop.

"Ain't that RaShawn and his scraggily butt?" Tafrica asks.

"With his sister. You know that can't be good." Wisdom nods with a somber tsking to her voice.

"Triple OG, low-key to the max," they say at the same time before slapping hands. They love to make up their own slang. If (though it's more like when) others start using it, they'll change it up. They also love drama, always wanting a front row seat to it, thriving on it like vampires in a blood bank.

Trailed by the twins, Nehemiah and I push through the crowd. RaShawn's sister's loud voice cuts through the chatter of the neighborhood. Her skinny body gestures and postures with much fury in exaggerated anger.

"Where he at? Where's the little bully?" she yells. Pink flip-flops match her sweatpants, the word "Juicy" bedazzled across her butt. A large set of lips paint her T-shirt like a giant, overlipsticked woman had kissed her chest. The girl towers over Moms.

"Get out of the street before you get hit. You know these fool drivers don't slow down around that curve." Moms prowls about the yard, her mere presence alone keeps everyone backed onto the sidewalk or edging the street. She remains unimpressed by all of RaShawn's sister's antics. Still, it's a good thing it's too early for her to have picked up my baby sister, Ahrion, from her school. It's harder to pull off being intimidating with an eight-year-old clinging to your leg. "There aren't any bullies around here. You need to calm your narrow behind down, coming up into my house like you got no sense."

"You need to get your hands out of my face." The girl steps backward. Her left hand on her hip, she raises her other hand to finger wag. The roar of the bus driving off draws her attention. "Look, there he go now."

I stop, my heart thumping in my chest, when I trace her gaze to Nehemiah. He often hangs with us after school until his mom, grandma, or whoever was staying at his house that week got home. Moms considers him a second son, which is good since he's like my brother. Moms took to him immediately. I don't know—it was something in his eyes, the same way you can find a puppy and know it had been hurt in the past. She understood that they may try to be the best puppy they could be, but something might set them off and remind them of the bad times. Her "adopting" him also had a downside since most folks don't realize just how protective Moms is of her children.

"I'm going to say it one more time: there aren't any bullies here." Moms is still in control, but I can tell she's reaching the limits of her . . . politeness. Like an engine revving into the red, each word spills out of her mouth pronounced with an edge. She might not want to admit it, but she's a lot like Nehemiah. Moms may be older, with a longer fuse, but once lit, she could go off like a Roman candle.

"He got in a fight with my little brother." The girl clutches RaShawn, waving him about like a prop doll. His sister is many things, concerned is not one of them. That girl can't find a maternal bone in a cemetery of mothers. This doesn't seem like a "no one messes with my brother except me" thing. She simply needs something to justify her storming around the neighborhood, an excuse to shout and remind everyone who *she* is.

Apology lights up RaShawn's eyes. He clearly regrets involving his big sister. That's not good for his look.

On his end, Nehemiah casually spits into the grass.

"Who? RaShawn? I heard about that. I handled it," Moms says.

"Handled it how? You ain't his momma," RaShawn's sister yells to everyone watching.

"I'm better than his momma. I'm actually here." Moms lets that line sit in everyone's ear for a minute, like she wants it to travel the neighborhood, before she continues. "And RaShawn, with his little wannabe hood self, gave as good as he got. *He* started the fight last week. Nehemiah and his angry excuse for a behind started it *this* week. I saw it, I stopped it. It got dealt with."

"Well, I'm here to see it gets dealt with better," RaShawn's sister blusters, but her voice falters a little bit, not quite convinced of her own words.

"And who. Are. You?" There it is. That vessel in my mother's neck throbs like it's keeping beat to that old jazz music she loves so much. She's on final countdown, soon to launch. "In fact, why am I out here explaining myself to a child? Someone who needs her own momma to do a better job of checking her hoochie outfits before she steps out of the house. You want things done better? Why don't you start by keeping your little hoodlum at home in the first place?"

"He over here 'cause everyone hangs out here." That's the second time RaShawn's sister checks herself. Her voice lightens up as if she is no longer sure of where to step.

"Not everyone. Not no more. He too through." Moms crosses her arms, a judge delivering her verdict. She stares down every kid present, daring them to say otherwise.

Sensing a change in the direction the wind is blowing, RaShawn's sister knows she's losing her audience. "That's fine. I'll just get my other brother and unleash him."

Uh-oh, I think. All a person has to do to jumpstart the fury in Moms is just hint at a threat to one of her children. The sky might as well turn faint green with the sound of a rumbling train in the distance signaling the imminent touchdown of a tornado.

Moms's brow knits. Her lips quiver. The large

veins in her neck tighten like thick cords. Her lips curl. Her body quakes. Moms's head ticks to the side. She starts reaching for her earrings, even though she doesn't actually wear any. Her eyes focus like a missile lock signaling "target: acquired" as she switches into a walking nuclear warhead scanning for a head to drop onto.

"Why wait? I'm right here." Moms slams her fist onto the hood of her car, buckling the old, paint-faded metal. Moments like this scare me. Not because I fear for my safety, but because in this state Moms is liable to do just about anything. As far as Moms is concerned, anyone can be a threat, so if the person is at least her height and in her face, they are danger enough for her to defend herself.

RaShawn's sister retreats a few steps, not quite wanting to turn her back on my mom. Better to just wander down the street with her butt intact. RaShawn's sister might have bark, but Moms has rows and rows of teeth. To save face, the girl mutters something loud enough to let everyone know she is still talking but incoherent enough to not draw anymore of Moms's temper in her direction.

"You got something to say? I can't hear you." Moms chops at her own throat with the edge of her hand acting like an ax head. "Here's my neck. Come on with it."

"Moms, she gone." I tug at her arm not wanting to make eye contact with her myself. The hope I cling to is that this scene has spent her supply of tactical anger. Otherwise, she might be too hot to charm at the moment. There's still a crowd gathered in our yard, but we have entertained them enough for one day. "Can we go inside?"

Tafrica and Wisdom grin and clasp hands like pleased diners pushing away from a buffet.

"What you all looking at?" Moms yells. "Show's over. Everybody off my property."

"What?" the twins say at once.

"Everybody. Out." Moms locks on to each of them with her "target: acquiring" gaze. The kids scatter, though they grumble with disappointment. On most days they know that Kool-Aid and pizza rolls await them at casa de Mitchell. They will probably take their frustration out on RaShawn tomorrow. Thems are the breaks for letting someone else handle your business.

"Here's my neck?" I ask Moms with the door barely closed behind us. "What does that even mean?"

She inhales and exhales deeply, like she's shedding a skin. Her mood changes and her face softens once the door closes. A couple jokes is all Moms needs to calm down. "I have no idea. I was in the moment."

"You were really feeling it." Nehemiah offers a crooked smile. Partly in sympathy, since he so often gets caught up feeling it, and partly appreciative of her "feeling it" on his account.

She plunks her purse on the counter and starts to riffle through the cabinets. "Look here, feelings weren't meant to be hidden behind walls. You need to bring out the right ones at the right moments. I'm grown and I'm still learning how to do this better, just so you know."

"You all overprotective," I say.

"Don't give me 'overprotective.' Other moms can

'not know' where their kids are, but I'm going to know. And you're going to know that I know. I don't care if I have to fight the whole neighborhood if that's what it takes to make sure you're safe." Moms whirls around and grips Nehemiah's head to drag him over. "That goes for your grapefruit-sized head, too."

Moms opens a few cabinets, spreading out bread and turkey and condiments, before stopping. Both her arms press against the counter like she's desperately trying to hold herself up. Then she starts talking.

"I remember when there were good days. Every day it seems like violence touches someone near us. Neighbors. Family. Friends. Even people that I don't know. But each one takes a piece of me. Every. Day. I don't know what to do."

Me and Nehemiah huddle near the kitchen, neither of us saying anything, because it's like she's not really talking to us and we don't want to interrupt.

"I go to work. I pay my bills. I make sure my kids are okay. I make sure they're respectful. I don't know what else to do. People want to say that mothers aren't taking care of their kids, but I'm out here taking care of my kids. I'm trying, but I'm also scared. There's so much violence out here. Around any corner. Any. Corner. Don't matter where you live. I just don't want anything to happen to my babies."

"It's okay, Moms." Not knowing what else to do, I reach my arm around her to give her a hug.

I think if Moms had it her way, she'd write me a letter—no, a book—with all her advice assembled in one place. And she'd fill it with things like I had to know when to leave "one world" behind to enter a different one. Like what it means to be us, not just how but when. Or how when I was at home, I had to "talk like I had some sense." All these rules to live by. Survive. Be . . . civilized. It sounds so complicated out loud, but in my heart I know what she means. She just wants to make life smoother for us and gets a little heated because she knows she can't.

"It's not . . . but it will be." She pats me on my back and wipes her eyes as she comes down, regaining herself. "I'm just tired of crying."

Moms finishes fixing the two of us turkey sandwiches. When we're done eating, she adjusts the front burners of the stove to let us roast a few s'mores over them. Once we wash up from being a gooey mess, we drop onto the couch in front of the television, ready to battle out a season of Madden on the Wii. I had just grabbed the remote to power on the TV when Moms snatches it and switches the Wii off.

"Now that we're all in a good place, you want to tell me what's up?" Moms scoots us down the couch to make room for her. Me and Nehemiah squish into each other, leaving a couch cushion between us and her as if the space of a cushion was enough to save us if she blew up again.

"The school call you?" I ask.

"Thanks for reminding me to check my voice mail."

Dang it. I kick myself for tipping my hand. Never give up information they don't already have. That is a straight-up rookie mistake. "Then what?"

"What do you think all them kids were buzzing

about? Was quick to run their mouths about what the principal had to say. Then that little so-and-so got in my face."

"No one knows what's up. All they know is that someone brought a gun too close to the school."

"I'll be talking to Mrs. Fitzgerald soon, don't you worry." Her already knowing also explains why Moms was so on edge and emotional. She doesn't like the idea of guns anywhere near us. She studies me first, then Nehemiah, then returns to me. I open my mouth to fend off the inevitable accusation when she cuts me off. "Well, I know it wasn't either of you two. Thelonius, you know I'd bust your butt two times if you even *thought* about bringing a gun up in here. And, Nehemiah . . . Lord knows you'd be waving it around showing it to everybody before you even made it in the door."

"That's what I'm saying!" Nehemiah yells.

"They rounded us all up anyway," I say.

"Guilty before proven innocent. You're caught in a bad place, between it being a prejudging world and you all being so proud to wear the reputation you have spent so much time and energy earning."

"It don't feel fair," I say.

"It isn't, but let's not act too innocent. Sometimes you have to look at the common denominator. You need to have a long talk with yourself. 'Self?'" Moms shifts her body to the side as if she's talking to an imaginary friend. "And then yourself says, 'Hmm?' So you tell yourself 'We've made some bad choices. If we continue to make bad choices, well, I don't know where we'll end up.'"

"You're silly." I relax a little, letting go of the arguments and stories my brain is furiously crafting to deflect her.

"While I have any say, you're going to be raised right and have all the opportunities to choose and do well. Have I mentioned that I don't care if I have to scrap with every raggedy person on the block? Or in your school? You two will always know that you had someone fighting for you. So no excuses."

She can be embarrassing sometimes. She loves to talk almost as much as Mr. Blackmon. But I think part of me needed to hear that me and her were cool.

My little antics aside, the thought of disappointing her with anything for real bothered me.

"Thanks, Moms," I say.

"Yeah, thanks, Moms," Nehemiah echoes with a smile on his face. He props his feet up on the coffee table.

"Boy, get those crusty shoes off my furniture and act like you've been raised with some sense." Moms swats his feet. "What are you going to do now? We can't have this cloud over my babies' heads."

I bend forward on the couch. "If I had to guess, we need to figure out what really happened. Try to clear our names before the school assembly. Because you know how they do with us."

"Need me to come up there and talk to your principal?" she asks. "It's probably only a matter of time before she wants to see me."

"No!" I say with a little too much force. I imagine Mrs. Fitzgerald and Moms both taking off their earrings, knocking over desks, and papers flying all over the room. "Not yet. I want to try to find out a few things first."

It was almost time for her to pick up Ahrion from the Applied Behavior Center, so Moms grabs her purse preparing to leave us to our games. "That's the son I've raised. Handle your business."

When life weighs on you, even the blankets become too heavy to move.

My alarm goes off ten minutes before Moms comes through to wake me up. Every morning, I hit the snooze bar before sparing a glance at the wrought-iron-framed picture of me and my dad. He left nine years ago. Moms gave the photo to me one year for Christmas. I can't remember the occasion that was worth us trying to preserve the memory. A candid shot of me smiling too hard and my dad with a soft frown (because he doesn't take pictures well, Moms says). The image has no memory in my heart, but it seems important to Moms for me to have it.

Maybe I need that fresh pinprick of pain to start my day. I plunge my head under the pillow to shield me from the inevitable. Moms flips on the light and bellows in her full singsong voice.

"Time to wakey, wakey, wakey!" She emphasizes each syllable of the last "wakey." She's been singing my wake-up call since the first day of kindergarten. It's old, annoying, and comforting all at the same time. "Do me a favor and make sure your sister is ready. It's almost time for breakfast."

I slip into my school uniform while still half asleep. I lay my clothes out every night before I go to bed so that I don't have to think first thing in the morning. Everything in my room is in its proper place—my trading cards in binders on my bookshelf, my Peyton Manning, Andrew Luck, and Russell Westbrook posters framed and on the wall with a carefully maintained layer of dust on the shelves and posters—so that I can tell if someone (either Moms when she's in trust-but-verify mode or, more likely, Ahrion) has been snooping in my room.

81

(It's not paranoia if they really are out to get you.)

Ahrion's room next door is a complete disaster area. Toys scattered all over the floor. Whenever she wants a particular toy, she tosses every other one out of her way until she finds it. Clothes thrown around the room in the same way. If you pay attention, you can see bits of order in the chaos. Her Matchbox cars organized by type and color. Her crayons and art pencils lined up by color, all sharpened to the same length. Her curtains flutter. A mismatched pair of shoes poke out from underneath them.

"I wonder where Ahrion is?" I sing out while circling the room.

"Here I am!" She flings open the curtains. Though eight years old, she likes her hair cut short, which makes her head appear too big for her body. She's darker than me, like Moms. Her eyes dominate her face. When she looks at you, you hold her full interest. Nothing distracts her from paying attention to just you. It's a little intense, but kind of cool, too.

"You're not very good at hide-'n'-seek," I say.

"You sounded worried. I didn't want you to be."

She runs to me and wraps her thin arms around me. She radiates such joy it's infectious.

"I will always worry about you. It's okay."

Some people treat her like she's broken. Moms explained what she has, something about being on the autism spectrum. I hear so many labels placed on me and my friends, I tune them out. All I know is that she's my sister. So she gets a little hyper sometimes. She doesn't always understand people. On the flip side, she doesn't grasp the idea of strangers. As far as she's concerned, everyone just needs a hug. If she's broken, I wish more people were broken like her.

I stand next to her loft bed. Before I can protest, rather than use her ladder, she scrambles up me. Two Matchbox cars rev to life—as she does a pitch-perfect imitation—and immediately crash into each other.

"Cars?" She invites me to play.

"No, Ahrion. We can't. Breakfast is almost ready."

She crosses her arms and lowers her head, but she can't maintain being pouty for more than a few seconds. "Only if you carry me."

"Fine." Before the word is fully out of my mouth, she climbs on my shoulders and I stagger down to the kitchen, weaving back and forth as I walk, the way she likes it. When we arrive in the kitchen, I freeze in the doorway. The sight horrifies me.

The electronic whine and drum snares burble along as a voice chimes, "'It's time for the percolator.'" Sliding along the linoleum, Moms lip-synchs the words into a spatula.

"No, no, no." I lower Ahrion to the ground and cover her eyes. No one should have to see this. My sister can't stop giggling.

"It's too late, son." Moms drops to the floor, one arm tucked behind her head, flapping, the spatula holding arm extended like she's a coffeepot about to take off.

"Oh. My. God. Mom, stop it!"

"What? Some people do yoga . . ." She bounces in place, still low. If she jumps up and says "drop it like it's hot," my day is done and I'm going back to bed. Thing is, this wasn't the worst I'd seen. If I'd heard

Boyz II Men or Jodeci playing, I wouldn't have even dared enter the kitchen. I can't deal with her doing full body rolls first thing in the morning. I shudder at the memory.

Moms has plates of food waiting on us. She enjoys the ritual of fixing breakfast. I scarf down the eggs (two eggs, always scrambled), toast (two pieces, always buttered, one with strawberry jam), and bacon (always overcooked because Moms is paranoid about giving her babies undercooked pork). She turns off the music and flips over to the *Today* show. "Homework check."

I open my planner for her to sign off on my homework.

"My turn," Ahrion says, so I hand her my binder. She draws a smiley face with extra bushy hair. "That's you."

"Thanks."

Moms hands me a book. *Langston Hughes: An Illustrated Edition.* "You have a week."

"Yes, ma'am." Moms "assigns" me books to read every so often. It's how I earn video game privileges.

Her library is full of books like this. With all the posters and paintings of Malcolm X; the Reverend Doctor Martin Luther King, Jr.; Sojourner Truth; Harriet Tubman; and Marcus Garvey hanging around the house, sometimes it feels like I'm living in a black history museum.

"All right, let's go." Moms grabs her keys and shoos us out the door. Moms doesn't want to leave me waiting at the bus stop without her hypervigilant supervision; she thinks it's better for me to get to school a half hour early. I want the independence of catching the bus. We split the difference: Moms drops me and Ahrion off at our respective schools on her way to work and I catch the bus home.

As we drive to school, I can't help but think that I really love Indianapolis. Sure, it's the only place I've ever lived, but this city is just so . . . me. Not so big that it doesn't still feel like a small town (we only have to drive ten minutes to find llamas, horses, and cows). Not so small that we escape big city problems. And the city operates like a gangster: it rolled up on all the towns surrounding it and straight took over. Take Persons, for example.

I read that Persons was a small farm town tucked into the northwest side of the city. When farmers drove their animals to the Indianapolis stockyards, they stopped in Persons. A railroad depot in the heart of the area gave it the "Crossing" part of its name. That was one story of how this area of town earned its name. Another version was that there was an important family named Persons who helped found the area. I really don't want to think that folks were so simple that just because people's paths crossed there, people literally decided to call the place "Persons Crossing." But that's the thing about Indianapolis, stuff like that just happens.

"You all right, baby?" Moms asks, interrupting my thoughts.

"Yeah. You know, school stuff."

"Remember, you can't count on others to protect your name. Only you can do that. You got this."

"Thanks, Mom."

"You got this," Ahrion echoes.

"Thanks, Ahrion."

The Persons Crossing Public Academy building mirrors all the schools in the district. A massive redbrick building broken up by tan concrete lines, its long drive in front forces parents to travel the length of the building to drop their kids off. I'm pretty sure they designed the walls to be so tall in order to intimidate the students, though it gave the building that much more of a prison look.

I close the car door behind me and take a couple steps toward school. I turn to wave bye to Ahrion, who enjoys calling my name until the car moves out of sight like I'm some gladiator heading into an arena. Rather than enter the school through the car drop-off door, I walk around to the side entrance. Key-card entry is required for all the entrances except during the morning arrival. Otherwise, people have to be buzzed in to report to the office. The way Persons Crossing is laid out, only one side has bushes. It has the added advantage of having little traffic over there since it isn't by the main, playground, or parking lot entrances, so there aren't any security cameras. But it does face Northwestway

Park. If someone was going to stash a gun in the park, they'd need to be able to retrieve it with as little notice as possible. The bushes create a natural barricade to hide shenanigans. I made a mental note of that for future reference.

Though the police are going to take any found gun seriously, it's not like they are going to go full-on crime scene investigation over it. Moms had her car broken into once and called the police. When they came to take the report, she showed them the broken window and told them she didn't disturb the crime scene in case they needed to dust for prints or run all kinds of tests we can't pronounce (Moms *really* loves those shows). The cops were like "ma'am, we don't do all that unless there's a body involved."

I'm not sure what I even hope to find. Maybe start here and trace my way back to the park along a likely route, see if I turn up anything. Perhaps scrounge around to see if anything is out of place. Lots of footprints have tromped back here. The early-morning light glints from something half buried in the dirt. A twisted bit of metal. I brush it off.

"What do you have there?" Marcel's voice scrapes my ears like manicured fingernails clawing my brain.

"Nothing. Just tying my shoe." I palm the twisted piece of metal, pocketing it when I stand up. On my tiptoes I can barely see over the row of hedges.

"Behind the bushes?" She saunters closer, just enough to not be overheard but still far enough away to not be associated with me.

"I'm a man who likes privacy."

"You a man now, huh?" She smirks. "You look like you're trying to pee back there."

"What are you doing here?"

"Thought I'd inspect the bushes, see if I can find some new friends."

"You all about making friends, huh?"

She doesn't fool me. She wants to throw me off my game. Either she wants to know what I know or she had the same idea I had about seeing what evidence was left. Her eyes don't flinch, and she studies me like a hawk about to swoop in. "Unlike you. I hear RaShawn's sister can get heated quick."

"Nothing but a thing." I shrug my shoulders.

"You have a good day. Be careful, though. I hear there might be some unsavory characters looking to bring in weapons."

Protected behind a glass case, trophies and awards and faded pictures of the school from back in the day hang next to a yellowed newspaper article detailing the opening of the school. I read it for the millionth time. Persons Crossings Academy has been around in one way or another since the early 1900s. From 1913 to 1938, Persons Crossings Elementary School began as a rural school that held grades one through six. I can't imagine what classes were like back then. A bunch of corn-fed farmer boys all in one room, smelling of sweat and cow manure, sitting around trying to stay awake after getting up at 4:00 a.m. to do their chores. They probably stared out a window daydreaming like I did when I was on the computer, except they didn't have the internet.

They also didn't need school. Their lives had already been scripted for them. They were going to be farmers like their daddies before them and their sons after them. They had little say in what they were going to be or what they were going to do. Their world decided that for them and expected certain things of them. Maybe that's why the school closed down when it did.

The article goes on to describe how the school switched to being a rooming house. Then a lawn mower repair shop. Then a grocery store. Then an auction house. Soon after, it was like people discovered the northwest side of town and the area suddenly boomed again and the district decided to build a new building. So in 2003, with a forgotten history and a name based on a forgotten area of town and a forgotten railroad, Persons Crossing Public Academy opened, this time housing kindergarten through eighth-grade students.

I lean against the glass cabinet and wait for the inevitable passing teacher to tell me to stand up straight and tuck in my shirt. Like I says, students and teachers all have their roles to play. Wrapping my hand around the bent metal in my pocket, like

I'm afraid I'll lose it, I cut to the head of the parade of kids lined up outside the cafeteria waiting for the eight o'clock bell to signal us to go to class.

When the bell rings, the other kids will run down the hallway, in a hurry for no reason. Rushing is its own point, I guess, one last release of energy and chatter before they have to be quiet and sit in their seats for the next six hours. But there's no rush for me. Only the slow walk down the long corridor few kids go down, to get to the room at the end of the hall that no kids want to enter.

There's no guilt or shame, though. It's my class. I am where I belong.

Going through the motions of being hungry, I grab a strawberry yogurt, a package of Teddy Grahams, and a container of apple juice from the cooler outside our classroom. Part of the free breakfast program—the district makes sure every kid has a balanced breakfast to start the day. No kid left behind or something like that.

On the second floor are the seventh-grade lockers. I spin my lock and open mine. A mirror greets me and I check my hair. Beneath it is a cup containing pens and highlighters. On the top shelf, what few books I need—since they have me mostly on computers—are stacked in a neat pile. Three rows of hanging shelves organize my folders. Taking the bare minimum I need for class, one folder and tucking a pen behind my ear, I close my locker and lean against it. I just manage to fit the straw into my apple juice when Nehemiah storms down the hall with a mean mug on, like he's mad at the air.

Nehemiah bounces his Teddy Grahams package off my chest. He hates them because he "never trusts anything that smiles all the time."

"Hey, T. What you no good?" We clap our hands, fire our guns, and snap our fingers as usual. From the jump, I liked Nehemiah. His confidence, his strut, his energy. Nehemiah knows who he is: one note, full volume, always. He has no pretenses about it. Sometimes I envy him that. Nehemiah glances from the unopened yogurt to my face. Twice.

I toss him my yogurt and open the second package of Teddy Grahams.

When he gets to his locker, he tugs the handle and it opens. He presets his locker so he can just open it when he's ready. It doesn't save him any time since he has to set the combination when he's done and he still manages to arrive to class late. Books and folders tumble out of his locker like they're doing a prison break. A tattered picture of Kevin Durant is glued to the inside of the door.

I check for any prying eyes before I reach for the metal bit and hand it to him. "I think I found something."

"Where'd you get this?" Nehemiah examines it in his palm.

"In the bushes. By where they say they found the gun. What do you think it is?"

"A tie clip, I think," Nehemiah says.

"Let me see." I snatch it back. Now that he said that, I can see it. A cheap tie clip.

"Ain't but one dude round here that'd wear something that corny."

"I'm just wondering what our next move should be," I say.

"Doesn't matter why. Like you say, they just going to blame us anyway."

"Yeah, well, just 'cause it's so don't mean it's got to sit right with me." I say, biting the head off another bear.

"Besides, what they going to do? Kick us out so we have to stay home and watch TV all day?"

"Mrs. Fitzgerald wasn't bluffing. She'll send us to Banesford, and that school don't play." I rub my eyes like I'm still sleepy. "We still got ten minutes before the bell rings. Want to chat with Pierce?"

"Man, I don't know if I'm up for his brand of weird first thing in the morning."

On our way to Pierce's locker, I notice all the attention on us. Eyes too careful not to make direct contact but still keep us in view. People moving out of our way. Nehemiah puffs up as we walk through the hall, but I don't enjoy it. Suspicion is one thing; fear of us is another.

The sixth-grade locker bays are on the first floor, as is the Special Ed room. Filled with the usual bustle and banter of, well, sixth graders. Excitement about an upcoming camping trip. Who's going to sit by who on the bus ride. The latest YouTube videos. The desperate panic over missing homework. Some still go on about the hottest Pokémon cards. They are so sixth grade.

It is no coincidence that Pierce has the last locker in the corridor. He paces in the center of the hallway. He walks around like a cowboy waiting on a duel partner. It is best to confront him before class, mostly because one never knows how he is going to react. I hear the teachers whisper about him when they think no one is listening. I know he has some "neuro" issue, and they've slapped him with every label they can think of, from ADHD to spectrum to initials I can't even guess at.

But he's in Special Ed. One of us.

"Hey, Pierce, hold up."

Pierce freezes in place like a statue, a knowing grin on his face. I step to his side, but he keeps staring straight ahead. His face is all hard angles and his skin ghostly pale. Up close, his lips are too pink and the edges of his eyes appear watery, like he suffers from allergies. The thing about Pierce is that he owns who he is. I am pretty convinced that he plays up his tics for effect. He's not dumb and knows that it gives him an advantage. People see them and think one way about him; meanwhile, he's really studying them.

I show him the tie clip. "Is this yours?"

I wait for him to pluck it from my palm. Instead, he tucks and withdraws his hand from his pocket and opens his hand, only coming up with lint.

"I think that's Pierce talk for 'It's mine,'" Nehemiah says.

Frustrated, I run my other hand through my hair. Pierce mirrors the gesture. When I step back and exhale slowly, he does the same.

"One can play at that game," Pierce says.

"Right. So were you behind the bushes?" I say.

"Let me think." Pierce strikes a new pose and taps his lip as if in deep thought. "Yes."

"When?"

"Last week. No, tomorrow. Sometime recent."

"Why we talking to this fool?" Reading my face, Nehemiah opts to provoke him. "He don't know nothing."

With those words, Pierce glares at Nehemiah, his eyes clear and focused with laser intensity. "I know many things. I'm not stupid."

I put up my hands like I'm surrendering. "No one said you were stupid. We just want to know when you were behind the bushes and if you saw anything."

"Or anyone," Nehemiah added.

"Only RaShawn," Pierce said.

"RaShawn?" I ask. "Why there?"

"It's where we meet. He gets me things."

"Like what?"

"Like noneya."

"Noneya?" Nehemiah asks before I can wave him off.

"None ya business." Pierce cackles, amused by his own joke.

I forgot how much that joke still circulated among the sixth graders. I step between them, hoping

Pierce will refocus. His attention span lasts until the earliest distraction. "How'd you lose your tie clip?"

"RaShawn got mad at me. Grabbed me by my shirt." Pierce imitates the action. He even reenacts the moment, mean mugging and staring us down with all kinds of evil eye. Well, as evil as Pierce is capable of looking. "Said I was making him look ridiculous and wasting his time. All I wanted was a frog."

"A . . . frog?" I ask.

"Yes. I would name him George. I'd get him a collar and a leash and take him for walks."

"I think we're about done here," Nehemiah said.

"Ribbit," Pierce says as we turn to leave.

We barely get out of earshot when Nehemiah asks, "What was that?"

"Pierce in full Pierce mode."

Pierce trails behind us, stopping with each passing girl to shout "Ribbit."

"I know he seems like he should be a suspect, but I don't know. He don't need a gun to get folks to leave him alone."

"Did he seem agitated to you?"

"He's always agitated."

"Maybe I'm imagining things. Still, he did tell us one useful thing. That the bushes are RaShawn's regular spot."

"You believe him?"

"It's something."

The late bell for homeroom rings. We spare a glance at each other before dashing to class, hoping to make it to our room's door before the echo fades.

Mrs. Horner scribbles the words "Do now" on the whiteboard along with instructions for the morning's busywork. She wants us to write a reflection essay on yesterday's events or, as she refers to it, "our dilemma." Someone must've gotten in her ear about it. And us. She doesn't name which events in particular, but Mrs. Horner rarely comes at things directly. She keeps things vague, saying that she doesn't want to limit our creativity. It's more likely that she wants us to accidentally tell on ourselves. Either that or she doesn't want to wind us up too much first thing in the morning. Like I said, busywork.

"What are you thinking?" Nehemiah leans over to ask.

"The way I see it, someone has to have a reason to bring a gun around here." Mrs. Horner hasn't taken notice of our conversation. I don't dare turn around to check Mr. Blackmon.

"Mrs. Fitzgerald named the reasons." Nehemiah began to quote: "'There isn't any reason to bring a weapon near this building. Not to impress anyone. Not to scare anyone. Not to threaten anyone.'"

"That's just it: impress, scare, or threaten. If Pierce was threatened, RaShawn may know something."

"That'd be a first. I've seen his grades." Nehemiah stifled a snicker. He spends far too much time hacking into the administration's database. "Still, I don't think he's going to be in a talking mood after yesterday."

"Let *me* worry about that. Can you arrange a meet?" I ask.

"For when?"

"Nine thirty. Middle of second period shouldn't be suspicious. So can you?"

"Let me worry about *that*." Since phones aren't allowed in school—if teachers see one they confiscate it and a parent has to pick it up at the end of the day—we have to get creative. Nehemiah scribbles on a piece of paper, folds it, and writes RaShawn's name on it before tucking it in his pocket.

I lower my head and pretend to work while he raises his hand.

"What, Nehemiah?" Mrs. Horner says without humor.

"I need to go to the bathroom."

"You just got here. Why didn't you go on your way to class?"

"It's an emergency." Those were the magic words. Teachers have to relent if the situation is an emergency. Even if they are suspicious, they can't risk a nervous bladder. All it takes is one student leaving a puddle under a chair for that teacher to visit Mrs. Fitzgerald's office to conference with angry parents.

"Fine. Mr. Blackmon? Can you escort this upstanding young gentleman to the bathroom?"

Mr. Blackmon slowly rises out of his seat, passing a skeptical glance from me to Nehemiah back to me. Twirling his water bottle once, he holds the door for Nehemiah.

Now, I've seen this play of Nehemiah's before. He'll go to the bathroom, waste a few minutes, and come out to grab a drink at a water fountain. Then without warning, he'll take off running, whooping and hollering. There's no way Mrs. Horner would ever catch him, having learned that the hard way, so she now has Mr. Blackmon do the escort. Nehemiah only needs a couple dozen feet to be able to duck into a room, stir up a distracting ruckus, and slip the note onto RaShawn's desk. Since Mrs. Horner will end up across from Mrs. Fitzgerald over it anyway, the cost of this stunt usually is detention for Nehemiah. And he won't be able to pull this again for a while because they'll be on guard against it for at least the next month.

Nehemiah's yelps echo down the hallway. I hide my smile by focusing on my work.

It takes a long time for Mr. Blackmon to return.

Without Nehemiah. He must've already been deposited at Mrs. Fitzgerald's office. Judging from the intensity of their conversation, Mrs. Horner blames Mr. Blackmon for not being able to control one of their students. A twinge of guilt washes over me. By the time the first-period bell rings, they are in their neutral corners.

I am the picture of a perfect student for the entire period, moving to the computer station to complete my math work without prompting. Teachers are like people: if you annoy them, by the time you need something they'll automatically say no just to spite you. Do what they want or make their job easier, they are quick to reward you. Checking the clock, I estimate the completion of my work to give me enough time to make it to the bathroom.

"Mrs. Horner, may I go to the restro—"

"No," she cuts me off. Mrs. Horner's not always like people.

"But I've completed all my work and I have to go really bad." This next bit costs me a bit of dignity. I bend my knees toward each other and cup the crotch of my pants. Mr. Blackmon shakes his head and upends his water bottle to his mouth.

"All right, but I'll escort you. No funny business."

"Yes, ma'am, I mean, no, ma'am."

RaShawn's footsteps echo from the hallway. He drags his feet, then stomps them like a zombie. His shirt is never quite tucked in, like he's always about to do some work. The sides of his head are shaved, but his hair is a series of short dreds in need of tightening that stand nearly straight up so it looks like he's wearing a fallen crown.

The bathroom door barely closes behind him when he leans against the wall, bored and impatient. I hate the fact that I'm doing the school's job for them. Still, it's my neck on the line and I'm not putting any part of me in the hands of teachers. Time isn't on my side. I need to do my thing.

"I didn't think you'd show," I say.

"Because of my sister? That wasn't on me. See, what had happened was—"

"I don't have the time. Consider it squashed."

"All right, then." RaShawn lets out his shirt and stands taller. "What's up?"

"You hang out at the bushes?"

"Uh-uh. You ain't pinning the gun on me." He throws his hands up in a "don't shoot me" pose. "What I need a gun for?"

"According to your sister . . ."

"I don't need a gun to deal with Nehemiah." RaShawn's voice thickens with anger.

With Mrs. Horner just outside the door, I pat the air, miming for him to lower his voice. "All right, let's say you don't. If you're doing business over there, it could be you on the wrong side of Marcel."

"Nope, try again. Me and the lady G have an arrangement."

"What kind of arrangement?"

"Noneya."

He must hang around Pierce a lot more than I thought. "Fine. You see anything or anyone suspicious?"

"Nah, bruh. I'm a blind man. If you looking for snitches, I'm out." With that, RaShawn bounces.

I wait a few minutes before leaving. While walking out, I fiddle with my belt for Mrs. Horner's benefit. "No one should go in there for a while."

"Your momma!" The words echo in the classroom and draw everyone's attention to Twon squaring off against Rodrigo. Barely half Twon's height and maybe a third his weight, Rodrigo is hopelessly outmatched. The whole scene plays out like a rabid rottweiler going up against an angry squirrel, yet Rodrigo can't help but keep running his mouth.

"I'm just saying, your feet stink." Rodrigo positions himself so that a desk blocks a direct route to him. As if a desk meant anything if Twon explodes. "We talked about athlete's foot in health yesterday. I'm betting that's what you have."

"Rodrigo, let it go and do your morning work. Twon, you're letting him take you out of your normal." Mrs. Horner sounds tired, like her own words bore her. Barely managing a glance, she doesn't bother to get from behind her desk. "You shouldn't let anyone have that kind of control over you."

"Besides, he a chipmunk," I add, less than constructively.

"Thelonius, you're not helping." Mrs. Horner narrows her eyes at me.

"At least my feet don't stink." Rodrigo studies Twon, waiting to see if he has room to push another button before he has to run. "You probably ain't got but three toes left. Fungus done ate up the rest."

This is what we do, mess with each other, like a battle rap without the rhymes. But the scene doesn't make me laugh the way it would have even a couple of days ago. Just like the ruckus in music class yesterday didn't, reminding me of eating candy you were so sick of even the act of chewing it became a chore. We're all a little on edge. Our jokes a little meaner or said with too much heat.

My mind shifts into overdrive. Rodrigo runs his mouth more, and in a more hurtful way, than usual. Maybe it's not as funny because it was one thing to joke when you didn't know better, a lot harder when you knew the truth. Twon didn't suffer from athlete's foot. I overheard Mr. Blackmon tell Mrs. Horner that he was planning on picking Twon up some new socks. Twon's family struggles. He wears the same pair of socks every day and they can't afford to do laundry regularly. Embarrassed by the state of his socks, Twon probably doesn't want to take off his shoes.

"Tell him he better keep my name out of his mouth." Twon balls and uncurls his fingers, testing his fists.

"Rodrigo, settle down. What did we just go over earlier this week about defusing situations?" His navy blue peacoat swinging over his left arm, Mr. Blackmon walks in without breaking his stride. His water bottle dangles from his right hand. His black sweater vest, with its red and white streaks, mutes the brightness of the red shirt underneath. His tie and pants repeat the color scheme. That man has too much time on his hands if he's going to coordinate his outfits like that. No wonder he often strolls in late. The situation fails to rush him to set his stuff down.

"I wish Twon would defuse his odor. I'm trying to do a public service," Rodrigo says.

That did it. Twon knocks over a desk and charges Rodrigo. Like I said, Twon is a gentle dude. He's always been big and the last person anyone would think to mess with. But he's also a little simple. One time he wore a pair of 3D glasses for sunglasses. Prone to daydreaming, he lives in his own world. He's real sensitive to folks making fun of him, especially if he thinks they are insinuating that he's not smart. Mr. Blackmon had given him a tennis ball to squeeze when he begins to get worked up or bounce when he got anxious. That ball was probably long thrown at Rodrigo by now.

Mr. Blackmon steps between the boys with the smooth glide of a soccer goalie blocking a kick. He looks a little too small to deal with Twon since they are about the same height. Twon knocks over another chair like Superman casually tossing a tank. He's pretty intent on smashing Rodrigo. Mr. Blackmon grabs him by his collar and drives him across the room before pinning him against the wall. The suddenness of his physicality puts the whole room on pause.

Pierce barely looks up from his desk. He keeps on snacking on Teddy Grahams while doodling on a piece of paper.

"Daaaaang!" Rodrigo applauds while jumping up

and down. "That was tight. Mr. Blackmon had to use his grown-man strength on him."

"Rodrigo, enough. One more word and you're walking the line for all your recess. For a week. Now, Twon, you need to calm down right now." Mr. Blackmon neither raises his voice nor uses any more force beyond enough to restrain him. Twon still needs a moment to catch his breath. "The whole reason you're in here and not with your class is due to the safety issue. You're too big to not be able to control your temper. You become a danger to others. Or, more important, yourself."

"Mr. Blackmon, there's not compliance with the instructions." Mrs. Horner stands up and sets her pen on her stack of papers. She's flexing her authority over him for our benefit. "His behavior warrants consequences."

"I understand that." Mr. Blackmon half glares back at her. You can tell he is starting to get irritated, but not at Twon.

"You have to start the process," she says.

Mr. Blackmon ignores her and continues to gently

talk. "Twon, you need to calm down."

"Mr. Blackmon." Mrs. Horner pushes her chair back as she points at the Scream Room. "You have to have compliance first."

"You're the one who wants him in there. Go ahead and put him in." Mr. Blackmon whispers but not loud enough for her to hear.

"*Now*, Mr. Blackmon," she says with steel in her voice. It occurs to me that she might still be heated over Nehemiah's stunt and her impending trip to Mrs. Fitzgerald's office and she's taking it out on Mr. Blackmon. And the rest of us.

Sheepishly, I slink back to my desk.

Mr. Blackmon escorts Twon to the Scream Room. He locks eyes with Rodrigo, as if asking "Are you pleased with yourself now?" For his part, Rodrigo lowers his head and refuses to meet anyone's eyes. He limps to the back row, his strut deflated. Folding his arms, he rests his head on them. Playing around and getting in trouble is just another day that ends in *y*. But getting someone sentenced to the Scream Room is dirty.

The process seems straightforward enough. The screamer has to demonstrate five minutes of "compliance." That means that they have to be quiet, have their back against the far wall, with the door shut. Only then could the timer start. Mrs. Horner used to have a rug and a beanbag chair in the Scream Room, but with the things that the kids did before they settled down—between the spitting and the . . . other stuff—I'm surprised men in those hazmat suits didn't have to remove them.

After the compliance, the facilitators have to fill out a reflection form. The reflection forms are used to monitor and chart behavior. "Behaviors" tended to escalate again when the kid is handed the form. It's like being forced to sit in jail, be released, and have to sign your confession. In the end it's all about the paper trail, and Mrs. Horner loves her paperwork. To calm them down afterward, the facilitator hands the students ten minutes' worth of busy work. Any violation and The Process™ has to start all over. The timer beeps as Mr. Blackmon programs it.

"You have five minutes, Twon," he says.

"I don't care." The boy tightens his arms like a wall in front of him.

"The shoes and jacket need to come off." Mr. Blackmon collects them but allows Twon to walk in on his own. "I can't have you hitting the door. Thank you."

You could have heard a cockroach skitter across the floor. The only sound is the thump from Twon as he bangs his head on the wall. "Stupid. Stupid. Stupid."

I can't tell if he's talking about Rodrigo, Mr. Blackmon, Mrs. Horner, or himself. Maybe all of them. Then comes the spitting.

"Wherever you're spitting, you're going to have to clean," Mr. Blackmon says.

"I don't care."

"You're just making more work for yourself." Mr. Blackmon leans against the door but refuses to look through the observation window. I always have the impression he hates seeing us locked up in any way. "I'm also going to have to let your mom know about this."

"If you're not going to follow directions, we're going to have to start the timer all over again," Mrs. Horner says.

Mr. Blackmon stares at her like she has lost her mind.

"I don't want to," Twon yells, his voice trailing as a *thwack* signals him dropping to the floor. Besides the sounds of thrashing as he probably rolled around on the floor, his next noises may have been sentences, but it sounds like he's being tortured. His screams are raw.

Don't ask me why, but this reminds me of church. Like when Mrs. Jenkins would get hit with the Holy Spirit. She would yell, sweat, fan herself, roll around on the floor, speak in tongues until folks could get her calmed down. No church I ever went to had a Scream Room.

"Nooo! I want to come out. I hate this school. I don't want to go here anymore!"

It didn't matter who it was—Nehemiah, Pierce, Twon, Rodrigo—they all read from the same script. Just last week, Pierce was in the Scream Room and yelled nearly the exact things.

Mr. Blackmon opens the door a fraction.

"Why you got to be so mean? To all the kids. It's not fair. You're all against us." Twon slumps over in a nod against the wall like a boxer who'd punched himself out. I'm not even sure who he's talking to at the end. Or what he's still fighting inside him. "My stupid brother. I'm the best in the world."

"Are you ready to come out?" Mr. Blackmon asks.

"Yes." Twon slurs his words in an almost sleepy voice.

Mr. Blackmon makes a motion toward the sink. It's all the excuse I need to get out of my seat. I grab the bottle of disinfectant and spray the Scream Room. Mr. Blackmon hands Twon a handful of paper towels. He wipes down the walls without complaint.

"Have a seat, man," Mr. Blackmon says. "You must have a hard time concentrating. Why else would you want to roll around on the floor?"

"I don't know." Twon crosses his arms and stares straight ahead.

"What'd you have for breakfast? You have the

chocolate milk? You have any candy this morning?"

"I don't know." Twon mumbles the words like a prisoner of war determined to recite only his name, rank, and serial number.

I hate that all I can do is watch. I hate the powerlessness of it all. My people hurting or hurting each other. I slump against the wall next to the Scream Room door.

"You need to be able to calm down. Get in some good learning." Mr. Blackmon squats in front of him so that they are at eye level. When Mr. Blackmon puts his full attention on you, he creates a bit of a spell, like one of those snake charmers or something. "What are you supposed to be doing?"

"Learning."

"How are you supposed to be sitting?"

"Like this." Twon swings one leg over the other and sets his palms on them.

"That's a good choice. And what should your mouth be doing?"

"Being closed."

"What if you have something to say?"

"Raise my hand."

"See? You know what you're supposed to be doing."

Mr. Blackmon bends over to Twon's ear as if to share a secret with him but instead stage-whispers. "Why you going to let some fool get under your skin? Once you start ignoring him, he's just a clown flapping in the breeze."

Twon smiles and relaxes. He cuts a hateful gaze toward Rodrigo.

"Look at me," Mr. Blackmon says. "You stay quiet, do a quick reflection form, I let you head to lunch ten minutes early."

"For reals?"

"Let's shake on it and make it real." Mr. Blackmon holds out his hand. Twon shakes it.

"Do you have this, Mr. Blackmon?" Mrs. Horner peers over her paperwork.

"Yeah, it's squashed. Knowledge is power." Mr. Blackmon keeps his back to her.

Knowledge is power. I pop the last Teddy Graham in my mouth and smile. Besides the twins, there was only one place to go if you want to know what's up with anyone. One person who is always dialed in to everything. One person who's haunting me like a bad rash.

Marcel.

I need to talk to the lady gangster.

Rules are in place for a reason. So we're told.

Rules create order. Rules keep everyone in line. Rules keep everyone where they are supposed to be. Rules make up the system, but no system is perfect. Given enough thought, everything breaks down, especially when stressed.

Stressing things is a specialty of mine.

The problem at hand is that I need to get from the Special Ed class to Ms. Erickson's math class where Marcel is. The hurdle isn't just getting over to Ms. Erickson's room but getting the opportunity and time to talk to Marcel without a lot of extra ears in our business. Sure, I can wait until recess, but where was the challenge in that? Besides, we only have until Friday, so each day, each hour, counts. I can't afford to waste any opportunity.

Rodrigo sits cross-legged in the corner behind Mrs. Horner's desk. He mumbles loud enough for everyone to know he's upset. Mr. Blackmon forces him write a reflection letter even though Rodrigo hasn't "done anything." In Mr. Blackmon's world, instigators are just as guilty as those who act out because "being in control of yourself includes your words."

Twon settles into doing his morning work, seething at the computer station, stopping just shy of cussing out the math problem on his monitor. Pierce approaches Mrs. Horner.

"Excuse me." Pierce clears his throat before he speaks, but his tone is well-mannered to a fault. "I need to go to Mrs. Wilheim's class to get the rest of my humanities work for the week. Would that be all right?"

"Have you read your book?" Mrs. Horner values

peace and quiet above everything else. Just like how some dads want to sit in front the TV and enjoy their show, and as long as the kids don't make a noise, they don't care what they do.

"I've finished all my assignments for the day." Pierce hands her a stack of papers, neatly folded. He loves to fold paper.

"That's fine. Mr. Blackmon, can you escort young Mr. Lyons to Mrs. Wilheim's class?"

"Mrs. Horner, I need to get my assignments, too." Whenever I try to polish my voice like Pierce, I always sound like a con artist on the prowl. Adults grow suspicious and know I am up to something, but they have no proof and need to see whatever I am up to play out. I might as well be a thief sending a note daring the cops to stop me from robbing a joint. I need to develop a new look, but for now, it works all the same.

As we walk by the different classes—language arts, humanities, art, science, Latin—students fill each room. Lined up and orderly, all attentive while the teacher speaks. Part of me wants to join them.

To be . . . normal, I guess. There are days I wish I fit in better and wonder what is wrong with me. It's like I have this voice that wants to tell me I'm broken. All right, sometimes that voice sounds like Mrs. Horner. Then there are the other voices, like Ms. Erickson.

Ms. Erickson is who I would have for homeroom if I weren't in Special Ed. Ms. Erickson is a math teacher. She always wears a huge smile on her face. She loves urging her students to talk in class. It didn't matter what her lesson plan was if a good idea popped up for the class to discuss.

Mrs. Fitzgerald left her alone because her students performed extremely well on the same standardized tests Ms. Erickson hates so much. That's the other thing about rules: success trumps everything. No one cares if you break them as long as you perform well.

Which is how Marcel flies under everyone's radar.

Ms. Erickson's class bustles with activity. The kids chat in noisy clusters, passing candy and money back and forth. Ms. Erickson perches against her desk like some grand, observant owl. She dresses like she finds her clothes at Goodwill. All her shirts have large, baggy sleeves. Whenever she walks between desks, all the boys perk up like prairie dogs trying to stare down them. Her hair bleeds from gray roots to darker hair to blond tips. She and Mr. Blackmon exchange a few words before he leaves. Ms. Erickson slides around her desk and punches my name into her laptop.

"Thelonius, you're doing well in your work over-all. Your actual class work is exemplary." She has the melodic voice of a bird high on hope. "Too bad we have those behavioral issues or you'd be doing perfect. We'd love to be able to have you in class."

"What are you guys doing today?" I observe the room while Ms. Erickson gathers my work. There are three or four centers of activity, each group congregating around a central person—Marcel Washington. She circles the room, checking in on each group, but not dealing directly with any of the activity.

In fourth grade, she experimented with the

nickname Marcy, but it never suited her, so she gave up on it. Her dad, a black dude, is a scientist who often visits her class to talk about his work. Her mom, a white lady, is the president of the PTA who also bakes a mean batch of brownies come school fund-raising season. If Marcel came from money, she never acted like it. Marcel always received straight As. By all reports, she was the best-behaved kid in the class. But I know better. The quiet ones are the ones everyone really has to watch out for. You see, an obvious stickup thug might get a wallet or two. Put them in bankers' suits and they were robbing folks for millions on Wall Street.

Marcel was strictly Wall Street.

"We're doing some lessons in applied economics." Ms. Erickson draws her long blond-tipped hair behind her ear and shoves her glasses farther up her nose. A touch of pride hints in her voice. "It's too bad you're not in here—I think you'd really enjoy this project. It was Marcel's idea. The kids are running little businesses. They're tracking inventory, setting prices, keeping ledgers, and even managing payroll accounts. I don't think they even realize how much they're learning."

"Can I watch?" I ask.

"Only from the back corner. I don't want you distracting anyone."

Like the lone guard of the cubbies, I wander toward the door. Her classroom theme centers around colleges. Banners from Indiana University, Purdue University, and Butler University; framed ones from Alcorn State, Wilberforce, Tuskegee, and Spelman.

"You have ten minutes to wrap up any transactions, then we transition into our university of mathematics portion of the day," Ms. Erickson announces. "Remember, I'm going to have to see proof of work before I let you get ready for . . ."

"Recess!" The class chimes in on cue. Like I say, just because you label something one way—like calling recess "enrichment" to make it sound more educational—doesn't mean it fools anyone into not recognizing it for what it is.

Marcel discusses a matter with Ms. Erickson

before meandering toward the sink, which happens to be right next to me.

"What you doing in here, Felonius?" Marcel says with her back to me. "Ms. Erickson could've run your assignments to you, so I figure you must want something."

I examine the door, one, to give the appearance of waiting for Mr. Blackmon, and, two, to keep my back between me and Ms. Erickson. "I wanted to check out your operation for myself. Been hearing things."

"What you heard about me?" Marcel sprays water into the sink, going through the motions of washing something out.

"I heard that your mom and dad weren't shelling out for an iPhone for you unless you earned the money for it yourself. I heard that you took your weekly lunch money and made a stop at the Dollar Store and bought candy and barrettes. You sold them and reinvested most of that money into more product, including mechanical pencils."

"Boys needed more stuff." Marcel pretends a

methodical search through the cabinets. "I never leave a customer base unserved or money on the table."

"Things took off and you franchised out. Got a few people working for you and everyone just pays you a cut." I lean against the cubby and stare toward the door. "And you do this under Ms. Erickson's nose."

"She's even a client. She bought her share of hair ties." Marcel chanced a moment to peek around the cabinet door to meet my eyes. "I see your boy, Nehemiah, has been busy snooping."

I ignore her all-too-accurate assessment. "That's a lot of money for product and cash to go through. How do you keep everyone honest? You have to have a way of making sure all of what's due you gets into your pocket."

"I've heard things about you, too." She starts organizing the shelves. "So you tell me."

I expected her to change topics. She's determined to test me. "What things?"

"You read a lot but funnel most of your energy into looking like you don't care about school. You have a bit of a paranoid streak. You're observant, good at reading people, and prone to sticking your nose where it don't belong whenever you get . . . bored. So what do you see?"

The kids wrap up their business, pocketing their candy. A few people write in notebooks and check their work with calculators. One kid lingers by the pencil sharpener opposite from us. Marquess Neal. "Kutter" to (what few people he called) his friends. His hair is a crown of twists, nesting baby snakes poised to strike. His eyes seem perpetually narrowed, like jagged scars. Not announcing his presence, he circles the room. Each student tallying their numbers notes him when he nears. He nods and they return to their work.

"Kutter keeps everyone straight," I say.

"You know that's right. He handles all my heavy work."

"Why does he work for you?"

"Because I'm a girl?" Marcel smacks her gum.

I play her game. "It's a lot to ask of some dudes, to report to a girl."

"Think he likes me?" She asks the question innocently, but I realize I'm still being tested.

"I don't think it works that way."

"Why does anyone do anything?" Marcel chomps on her gum, sounding like a cow making a mess of cleaning cud from its mouth. She purposefully designs her act for maximum annoyance. "Because there's something in it for them."

"Money?" I shrug.

"Deeper than that."

"I don't get it." I shift toward her, careful not to give the impression that we might actually be talking.

"No, you don't. You have a 'moms' who thinks the world of you. You have teachers like Mr. Blackmon who believe in you. And you got friends like Nehemiah who are ride or die with you. You're rich compared to most folks."

"It's that deep."

"It's that deep. Be careful not to drown." Marcel emphasizes the words to remind me of my place in the greater order of things. She shuts the cabinet door.

I already regret this. Marcel likes to play games too much. One of those people who believes themselves smarter than everyone else, she's so confident about that fact she never bothers to particularly hide it. Instead, every conversation becomes a maze where she jogs several steps ahead of you. I don't know who's more exhausted after each interaction, me or her.

On the watch for Mr. Blackmon, I calculate how much time I have left for this dance with Marcel. It's past time to get down to business. "You know about the gun?"

"What about it?"

"I'm trying to find out who brought it."

"Why? You decide to go into the snitching business?"

"Why does it got to be like that?" The accusation hits harder than I expected it to. I'm not about to be out here snitching, but I don't know if this falls into a "no snitching" situation. Taking a sudden keen interest in the decorations in case Ms. Erickson watches, I adjust one of the university banners. "Now who sounds paranoid?"

"Because you asking a lot of questions about stuff that isn't any of your concern."

Kutter scrapes his chair along the floor tiles. It draws everyone's attention, but he only eyeballs me. Forming a peace sign with his fingers, Kutter points them first at his eyes, then toward me. Subtlety isn't in his skill set. Employing Kutter is like having a hammer as the only tool on a tool belt. I can definitely picture him with a gun, but I play things cool.

"You know how it goes, Marcel. Folks have made it my concern. This will come down on me and Special Ed."

"You stay true to your crew. I respect that." Marcel blows a large, slow bubble, lets it pop, but brings the mess back into her mouth with methodical ease. "Just as long as you understand that you aren't untouchable. Handle your business. You just make sure that it's only *your* business you're handling."

"You threatening me, Marcel?" I watch her like an insect I suspect might be poisonous, wondering just how far Marcel might go to "handle her business."

"Absolutely not." Suddenly I wonder if I sound so phony and grating when I put on my all-too-innocent routine. "If I were you, I'd look to those closest to you first. I'm telling you that as a courtesy. Consider it a respect thing. Game recognizes game. Just also understand that snitches get stitches."

We have to learn our numbers, and today's lesson of the cafeteria involves division.

Kids march through the hallways arranged by classrooms. The boys of Ms. Erickson's room, full of too-conscious swagger, acknowledge Kutter for permission before play punching one another. Even more than Ms. Erickson, he controls the line with his uneasy menace. Those locked out of his crew face a vague powerlessness. They keep their heads down, hoping to not be noticed. The idea is that the eighth graders would mentor the sixth graders as to the ways and culture of the school. It's like having short-timer inmates school the new ones. The classes arrange themselves around specified tables, boys tend to be on one end, girls on the other. Clusters of friends, alliances of interests, all fall along invisible boundaries.

The cafeteria lady hits my tray with a heavy dollop of hash browns. Breakfast for lunch is usually the biggest hit of the week, second only to pizza days. French toast, hash browns, and sausage patties, all are gobbled down in a greedy blur. The carton of milk weighs the tray down, throwing off my tray's balance so it requires both hands to carry. It's hard to pull off cool while struggling to keep a tray straight, so I hustle to my seat.

"You going to eat those?" Crumbs dust Nehemiah's mouth and shirt.

"Nah, go ahead." I slide my plate to let Nehemiah take my French toast sticks.

"There you go thinking again. Ain't you had enough of that? You making yourself sick." Nehemiah's tone sounds almost like a mother's. Concern isn't a muscle he regularly exercises. Having eaten all his scavenged food, Nehemiah now outright picks at my tray since I obviously show little interest in it.

Twon receives a triple portion of food. The lunch lady happens to be his aunt and is generous with his portions to begin with. Mr. Blackmon nibbles from a container of carrot sticks and a Baggie of pumpkin spiced granola. We turn our noses up at it when he offers some.

The Special Ed students are allowed to be with our classes during lunch and enrichment. Most times we choose to take our lunch back to our class-room. If we are going to be designated "special," we are going to take full advantage of that status, flipping things so that it's a privilege. In our room, we can talk freely the entire period, unlike the regulated cafeteria where students had to be quiet except for the final ten minutes of lunch, when they are free to chat. Today I convinced everyone to eat in the cafeteria (so that I can observe people, but I leave that part out).

The school cafeteria doubles as the auditorium, so there is a raised platform that can be closed off by the thick burgundy curtains. Me, Nehemiah, Twon, and Rodrigo sit around a table on the stage. The perfect perch from which to see how the different players operate in their natural element.

"What do you see, Thelonius?" Mr. Blackmon wanders over. The way he watches me watching folks annoys me. His scrutiny makes it hard for me to focus.

"What do you mean?"

"When you look out at the rest of your class, what do you see?"

This time of day is the toughest for teachers to corral us. All our energy builds up to this point and we tick away the minutes all morning, waiting for release. Whatever tattered bits of discipline remain in us fray to shreds and the teachers resign themselves to managing the unruliness. We outnumber them.

There are perfectly valid reasons to be scared of spiders, just not the ones people typically think of. The number of spiders should make folks break out in cold sweats. Numbers can tell an interesting story. Spiders are in just about every home, to the point where you're never more than a few feet from a spider whether you can see them or not. The larger ones can feed on lizards, birds, and even small mammals. If you were to add up the weight of all the spiders in the world, it would come to 25 million tons. Combined, they eat between four hundred and eight hundred million tons of prey in a year. If you add up the weight of all the adult humans on the planet, it comes to about 287 million tons. In other words, the sum of all the spiders could eat all of us and still be hungry come snack time.

The numbers don't lie, but you can make them tell whatever story you want.

Having drawn the short straw today, Ms. Erickson's been sentenced to lunch duty. She patrols up and down the rows of tables with a soft glare on her face meant to silence any stray whisperers. She places orange cones on the ends of each table, signaling silence to allow the students "the proper concentration" to finish their lunches. On days like breakfast days, we accomplish that task within minutes. The only people still eating are those who suffer through home-packed lunches of cold SpaghettiOs, stale chips, and peanut butter and jelly sandwiches (especially since the jelly had all morning to soak through the bread). Some kids open books and duck their heads to pass the remaining time. Others fidget, barely able to contain their anxious energy. A few slip out their cells, keeping them out of the eyes of teachers since phones are "forbidden." Everyone competes to get away with as much chatter or game playing as Ms. Erickson's back allows.

I focus on Marcel. She looks around as if her name was called and flashes a crooked yet toothy smile at me. Without turning from our locked stare, she bumps Kutter to gain his attention. The two of them sit on the dividing line between the boys and the girls. She raises her carton of milk but doesn't take a drink, instead using it to block her lips from my view. She needn't have bothered because I suck at reading lips. Kutter bobs his head, a wry sneer spreading across his mouth. He smothers a laugh. Glaring at me gives me the gist of whatever flutter of conversation they exchange. Marcel tips her milk toward me in mocking toast.

"Sheep and wolves," I say finally.

"Which are you?" Mr. Blackmon asks.

"Neither." I'm not someone who follows what everyone else does or tries to hide unnoticed. But I'm not going to hunt my people and gobble them up, either. I'm something else, I guess.

"How do you think they see you?" Mr. Blackmon picks out a carrot stick with great flourish to allow a moment for the question to sink in. I know his little tricks.

I mull Marcel's words, churning them in my mind over and over again, trying to make sense of them. Look to those closest to me? Nehemiah, Twon, Rodrigo? There's got to be a clue in there somewhere. Or maybe a warning. This may all be part of her game. Get my head spinning so that I'm too caught up to catch whatever she's up to.

"A lion," I say finally. "The other wolves play at being bad, but they're scared that I can come down at any time and hunt any of them."

"Is that how you see yourself?" This is what I mean. Mr. Blackmon just can't help it. Every conversation transforms into an opportunity to push into me. He's a walking, talking after-school movie intent on teaching me something. The level of concern almost suffocates me and makes talking to him too intense, almost a drain, and I need to concentrate.

"Mr. Blackmon, you need more than carrots in your diet," I say.

"Okay, I get the message. It's just you reminded me of something. You ever watch Road Runner cartoons?"

I perk up a little. "Yeah. Sometimes they run those old cartoons on the Cartoon Network."

"Uh-huh." Mr. Blackmon takes the dig in stride. "Every so often they show episodes that didn't focus on Road Runner but on Wile E. Coyote and Sam Sheepdog."

"Actually, it was Ralph Wolf. They just drew him like Wile E. Coyote."

"What have I told you about sentences that

143

begin with 'actually'? No one likes a know-it-all."
Mr. Blackmon's glasses slip down his nose. He
straightens the seam of his sweater vest. "Anyway, *Ralph*"—Mr. Blackmon emphasizes the noted
correction—"and Sam were both on the clock, each
had a job to do. Ralph's was to catch the sheep; Sam's
was to protect the sheep. They weren't mad at each
other; they were just being true to their natures."

"What's that got to do with me?"

"This is my long-winded way of agreeing with
you. I don't see you as a wolf or a sheep either. You're
a good kid, even if you don't always believe it. I'm
going to be straight: you might even have a hint of
wolf in you, but in your heart, you're still more . . ."

"Sheepdog?" I shake my head.

"Look, this sounded a lot more cool in my head."
Mr. Blackmon tips his water bottle to his mouth.

The lesson of recess is controlled chaos.

The day builds to the moment we pass through
the double doors that open to outside. Outside is our
world. It begins as soon as Mr. Blackmon stands to

escort me, Rodrigo, Nehemiah, and Twon. Whether by design or by negligence, enrichment time seems like yard time in prison.

In order to maintain the illusion of control, the rule is that the students have to continue "personal discipline" until we reach the end of the sidewalk. Ten steps count down the long march to freedom. Eyes widen and dart about. Coats zip up, miniature knights donning their armor in preparation for the combat we call play. Our pace quickens, excited hops peppering our footfalls, but not quite running because we'd be sent back to the door to "try it again." As a crush of bodies, we surge forward without shoving because that, too, would get us sent to the back of the line.

Three steps.

Two.

One.

Crossing the line, we explode in screams despite the "no yelling" warnings of our teachers. Peals of laughter and whoops follow as we chase one another. The playground erupts in a tempest of activity.

Rodrigo assumes his usual post, walking the line surrounding the basketball court. He earned ten minutes of time-out for running his mouth to Mrs. Horner and she always collects.

"I got something on Kutter." Even with the bright sun, Nehemiah draws his jacket tight around him. Besides being able to get into the school administration's computer system whenever he wants, Nehemiah can go places I can't and talk to people who won't talk to me. Apparently my mouth burns a lot of bridges and, hard as it is to believe, some people consider me a know-it-all jerk.

"You peek at his records?"

"Thought about it. RaShawn, too. Teachers around here don't guard their passwords or laptops for anything. But I didn't need to. I just started asking around. Word is that Kutter has folks terrified."

"Makes sense. He used to squad up with Nyla," I say. Like Marcel, she's part of the power group that basically runs the school. "Then he went solo. Thug for hire. Especially when we start looking at motive: either who would want to bring a gun to school or why would someone need to bring a gun to school. This puts Kutter at number one."

"So what do you want to do, T?" Nehemiah asks.

"Give me a sec. I have to talk to a couple folks."

"Want me to come along?"

"Yeah," I say, but I don't know why. Something didn't sit right with me, one of them bad feelings, like the weight of eyes on me. "Discreet, though. Watch my back."

We head toward the far side of the blacktop. A fence topped with barbwire lines that edge of the school's property line. A stand of trees grows on the other side, their branches shadowing that corner. The twins hold court in the shade like it is their own private tree fort. Most days, I never give a second thought to either Tafrica or Wisdom. I call myself "not wanting to be distracted by no females."

"What's good, Thelonius?" Tafrica says.

"You look ill, T." Wisdom adjusts her glasses. I notice her braces for the first time. She's the only person I've met who can pull off pigtails, braided or otherwise. "Like something a cat threw up."

"I must be coming down with something," I say.

"What's your friend doing? He acting all suspicious over there, trying not to be noticed," Tafrica says.

Nehemiah lingers by the edge of the building, between the spontaneous game of soccer and our conversation.

"He good," I say.

"What'cha need, then?" Tafrica says.

"I just want to know a little bit about Kutter."

Both Tafrica and Wisdom check around for prying ears before both grab me and yank me close.

"What are you asking about him for?" Tafrica whispers through clenched teeth.

"What? I just want to know how he connected with Marcel."

"Who said they're connected?" Wisdom asks. She doesn't quite huddle with me and Tafrica but keeps her head up in a constant scan of who might wander too near.

"You're kidding, right? Everyone knows he works for her."

"But no one asks."

"I heard he's homeless," Wisdom says.

"Homeless?" I ask.

"Couch surfing with relatives. No one wants to take him in for too long. Did a stint in one of those juvenile boot camp type places. The Change Academy, I think."

I have a theory that everyone loves to stick the word "academy" in a school's name to make it sound more prestigious. Though I suppose if you call schools what they were, "Whoop That Trick" Academy doesn't have the same ring as the Change Academy.

"Only a rumor." Tafrica's head snaps in Wisdom's direction. "We don't do rumors. Especially about them. That's dangerous. If Kutter broke from Nyla and if he went to work for Marcel, it means there's trouble among the Queens. We too close to them and we ain't trying to get caught up in that mess."

"Becoming collateral damage isn't good for my look." Wisdom nods.

"He straight hood, that's all you need to know."

"Okay, I got it." I lift my hands and back up. That's when I feel it. The weight of eyes tracking me. Doing a quick scan myself, I have no idea from where.

"Word of advice, T," Wisdom offers. "Be careful who you ask about."

"Or to who," Tafrica continues. "You never know who's listening or who they loyal to."

I rejoin Nehemiah. "We good here."

"Learn anything?"

"I'm not sure." I swat him in the gut and nod toward the court. "But I'd really like to play basketball."

"We're coming in." Nehemiah shucks his jacket as we jog over, stopping the action on the court.

The teams switch around so that Nehemiah, me, and Twon can be on the same squad. Kutter and RaShawn are on the other side.

A few times up and down the court has me pouring sweat. Some kids still cling to hoop dreams, running across the court like LeBron James commanding the floor—their eyes full of cool indifference when we join the game—oblivious to the fact that most of us are weak ballers. That some are chubby or that some are scrawny. That some are tall while others could not reach the bottom of the net no matter how hard they leaped. It doesn't matter how much skill you have: playing the game is the point.

I grab the rock at the top of the key. I dribble with a wary trot, allowing the teams to get used to one another while I study how they move. With a hot spin to my left, I bring the ball back right. Twon undercuts his man, finding some space.

"I'm open," Twon yells.

I wave him off and fire a pretty fadeaway jumper. I *know* I look like Steph Curry stabbing a dagger in the heart of the opposing team with a last-second shot.

"Check it up top." I raise my hands in anticipation of the ball.

"How come?" RaShawn asks.

"We're playing make it, take it."

He skulks over to set Kutter up to drive. I intercept a sloppy bounce pass. Spinning around past Kutter, I evade the sea of elbows and smacking hands, leaving the other team behind. I rush the backboard without dribbling, blasting off to the rim, flying as high as my body manages. Though falling three feet short of touching any part of the rim, my imagination fills in the rest. I act like I'd just dunked on someone. Today is my show.

"I'm out, man," Twon says.

"No one likes a quitter, Twon," I remind him.

"No one likes a no baller either. You never pass the rock." Twon waddles off the court, toward the playground equipment in search of a game of tag or something to jump in on. He doesn't bother to turn around. Waggling my head back and forth, I imitate him saying, "No one likes a no baller either." I kick a pebble from the court in his general direction.

His words sting, though. No one wants to be seen as a black hole: where once the ball goes in to him, it never comes out. Nor do I want Twon to leave. I just want to win. When the ball isn't in my hands, when I'm not in control, I'm helpless. I can run around all I want, make screens, confuse the defense, but the reality is that whoever has the ball determines the action. Plus, I don't particularly trust my team-mates. Tucking the ball to my side, I watch in silent protest. This is as close as I'm going to get to apologizing. It's not like I can announce in front of the other team that I'd pass the ball more.

Split between having to watch Twon, Rodrigo, and us, Mr. Blackmon positions himself by the other set of doors closer to the eighth-grade wing. Marcel switches positions with him, stationing herself by the doors closest to the cafeteria.

I pass the ball to Nehemiah on the next trip down the court.

"Guard the rock. Guard the rock!" I scream, but RaShawn quickly strips Nehemiah of the ball. Going for an easy layup, he pays no attention to the galloping footfalls chasing him. I catch up from behind and swat his shot out of bounds.

"He vandalized you!" Nehemiah yells, feeling avenged. "He schooled you, son."

Kutter glances over toward the cafeteria doors.

Marcel nods.

Nehemiah checks the ball up top. RaShawn

tosses the rock to Kutter.

"Show *me* what you got." Kutter flashes a humorless grin. Dribbling the ball twice, he pounds the ground with it. Regripping it, he presents it to Nehemiah. Daring him.

I step toward Nehemiah to check the ball for him, but he brushes me back. I was about to insist but think better of it, not wanting to accidentally punk him. There are rules to the game. Once challenged, Nehemiah can't back down or he'd be seen as soft or weak. He wouldn't be able to play out here if he gets that rep. Or worse, he'd have to do something stupid to shake it. Kutter lobs Nehemiah the ball. Stretching his long arms out, Kutter crowds him. Nehemiah doesn't have a natural game. He dribbles with a heavy hand, thinking too hard about where the ball lands. Slamming it on the concrete, he moves like a sleepy elephant.

Nehemiah throws a head fake, which fools no one, and drives to the basket. Kutter's elbow crashes into the side of his neck when he jumps up. I spring to Nehemiah's side, one shoulder braced toward him to hold Nehemiah back just in case.

"What the hell?" Nehemiah touches his neck, checking his hand for blood.

"All ball," Kutter says.

"You going to mug me every time I drive?" It's a simple question, but I didn't trust the way Nehemiah's head ticked to the side when he asks it. I recognize those eyes.

"If you're going to cry about it, take it." Kutter tosses him the ball.

"No foul. You can have it." Nehemiah flings the ball to him. Hard.

All eyes land on Kutter. He catches the ball completely unfazed, not bothered by Nehemiah's anger. He plays to get into Nehemiah's head. Nehemiah provides an easy target for that kind of plan. In that way, he is the weak link on the team.

Kutter does his strong crossover again. He waits for Nehemiah to not only come for him but commit. Even Twon, from the other side of the playground, would have seen Nehemiah planting himself in position to knock Kutter to the ground on his drive.

Kutter uses his crossover move to evade Nehemiah. But Kutter doesn't take the easy shot. Going from up top, he lobs a floater of a pass. Easily intercepted by Nehemiah, the play is sloppy. Too sloppy. Like he wants to give Nehemiah another crack at him. I push off my man to gain some room. Nehemiah can kick the ball out to me. Two defenders, two of Kutter's crew, block my path. Like the steel jaws of a bear trap slamming shut, I piece together their play too late.

Nehemiah drives down the court through a clear lane that opens up for him. Bait he's unable to resist. I call out to him. Kutter steps into the lane, just enough to trip him. Nehemiah sails through the air. He hits the concrete and rolls to a stop. The ground rips up his shirt and cuts a seam across the knees of his pants. Kids rush over to pick him up, but he knocks their hands away. An empty hardness fills Nehemiah's eyes. The same way Moms ticked once her needle crept into the red and was beyond hearing anybody.

Nehemiah springs up and charges. Kutter waits

on him. His boys part to open an unobstructed path for Nehemiah to reach Kutter. A bubble of bodies collapses on them after that. Only then do I realize that we have no allies in the group. Rodrigo's still walking the line. Twon is on the other side of the playground along with the all-too-far-away Mr. Blackmon. Ms. Erickson patrols the swings, attending to the gossip girls. We are all alone.

I freeze.

The scene rewinds itself and replays at slow speed. I can't breathe. Fear creeps up my belly and down my legs, rooting me to my spot. I'm smart and I'm tough, but I'm not hood level. I wasn't raised in the streets. Kutter's stone-cold glare, its sheer ruthlessness, chills me. It's the stare of someone with nothing to lose. That there are few lengths he isn't willing to go. Nothing he wouldn't sacrifice.

All his rage and hate and emptiness could just as easily land on me. His hands could easily hold a gun. In a moment, his gaze burns through me and reveals how little I understand what all is in motion. It reminds me of what I do care about and how much

I have left to lose. Starting with my friends.

Though they anchor themselves in a pretend pick-and-roll to block me, RaShawn and his partner don't have to do much work. The boys surge, a storm on two fronts: one carefully positioned to shield prying eyes, the other pounces on Nehemiah. Their bodies press in. They shout in angry snarls. Bits of spit fly as they work themselves up. Not so loud as to draw too much attention. The boys close in tighter. Quick jabs to Nehemiah's gut. An elbow to his jaw. A few well-placed kicks turn to stomps when he stumbles to the ground. Kutter grabs Nehemiah's wrist and falls on it. A wet pop follows along with Nehemiah's howl.

"Step back, step back." Mr. Blackmon charges through the boys. "Give me some room."

Kutter is slow to roll off Nehemiah, who squeezes his eyes shut, making a dam of his eyelids. Heavy tears stream down his face, mixing with the dirt on his cheeks to create muddy streaks. Mr. Blackmon checks him for cuts and bruises. When he touches his arm, Nehemiah screeches again. The gathered crowd swells. Some have the decency to wear horrified expressions. Though they fight for a better view, they leave a curious space around me, allowing me plenty of room. Or distancing themselves to not catch what I have: a case of traitor for not jumping in to defend Nehemiah.

Kutter strolls past me. He whispers, "You in *my* yard."

"Come on, Nehemiah, we're going to the nurse's office." Mr. Blackmon scoops him up as best he can to help him to his feet. "Can you walk?"

Unsteady at first, Nehemiah backs away from Mr. Blackmon to favor his hurt wrist. "It wasn't my fault. They started it."

"You can sing that song to Mrs. Fitzgerald." Mr. Blackmon stays near to steady him in case he needs it. "The boys who came to get me say you were the one shoving folks."

"It's not fair." Nehemiah kicks over a trash can on his way in. The movement shoots an arc of pain through his arm because he cradles it more.

Ms. Erickson arrives to shoo the kids back to

their schoolyard distractions. The boys stagger back toward the court as if awakening from a deep sleep. Their game starts off sluggish, but within minutes finds its rhythm again. Without me.

Sucking on a Blow Pop, Marcel sidles up next to me.

Withdrawing the lollipop from her mouth, she gestures toward the building. "Your boy's off to see Mrs. Fitzgerald. She don't play when it comes to blacktop tussles."

I don't respond.

"Looks to me like you out here all alone. Your crew, well, they ain't much. A lot of talk but they got no heart. Now, my crew? They're loyal. They're soldiers. They know how to get things done. I know a mind is a terrible thing to waste and all, but I want you to think about that and how easy it'd be to get got before you go asking any more questions."

A funk settles on the Special Ed room.

Everyone acts restrained, like someone has died. The mood matches the awkwardness of settling back into anything approaching discipline and self-control. Like a bunch of zombies, we quietly stumble through the day, barely going through the motions of getting our afternoon work done, powering our way to dismissal. Nehemiah being absent doesn't fully explain the lack of energy. I struggle to find a word to describe the emptiness.

With Pierce off in art class, Rodrigo drags his desk to the back corner to distance himself from

Twon. They both read to themselves. Rodrigo opens a book on his desk, but plants a comic book within it. He's so committed to beating the system that he forgets that he could have just chosen to read the comic out in the open, because no one cares what he reads as long as he's reading. And more important, quiet.

I tilt my chair on its back legs. Tossing my book so that it spins in the air, I wait for it to slam when landing spine-side down against my desk. The clatter breaks the tranquility of the room. I'm mad because I'm frustrated and humiliated. For all my talk and rep, I got caught cold when it was time to fight. I felt powerless because everything was overwhelming. It occurs to me that Nehemiah may feel that way a lot. The feeling fuels his anger. But when my mind drifts to my friend, my mood spirals farther into a dark place.

The events of recess and the aftermath play like a movie on a loop in my brain.

After the bell, me and Twon have to walk back to the Special Ed room with no escort. The other middle school classes line up, waiting for each of their teachers to lead them inside. They allow me and Twon to enter first. I step between the lines. The big kid from music class, Jaron, plows his shoulder into me when I walk by. I turn to glare at him but spy the wall of kids behind him. There's no warmth, and barely any recognition, in their faces. I stand accused. Twon scurries off to class, but I stop for a drink of water. I refuse to let them think that they are getting to me. When the other classes catch up to me, another wall of glares meets me. The whispers soon start.

"Snitch."

"Snitches get stitches."

"Principal's boy."

"Snitch bitch."

They have Marcel's fingerprints all over them to keep me from finding out what happens and why. The rumor will carry weight because you never side with administration. Ever. There are rules to this game. Kutter and RaShawn especially enjoy spitting out the words. The other boys rise in chorus, not

163

bothering to whisper.

I have to poop. The door to the bathroom opens, its light orange walls visible before wrapping around a blind corner. Teachers rarely enter the student bathrooms. The wall blocks the casual observer. Peals of laughter or muffled cries echo like the same brand of bathroom shenanigans. I decide to hold it rather than chance literally being caught with my pants down.

"You going in or just standing there sightseeing?" some kid asks on his way in.

The door opens again. The flash of brick walls. The choking of the sounds when the door closes. I picture myself outnumbered and overpowered out of the protective sight of a teacher. I remain rooted to my spot, just like I was when Nehemiah was in trouble.

Later I find the note on my desk, and I feel like a coward all over again.

Someone scrawled the word "snitch" on it, with a drawing of a decapitated head beneath it. Pencil shades in a black eye and scars along the face. I fold

the note back up. The thought of throwing it away
makes me mad. I might as well toss my hands in
the air in the final act of surrendering. To admit I
am weak, vulnerable, and soft. But they're right. I
shove the note into my pants pocket. I know it's not
just my name I'm trying to clear and keep anyone
else from being hurt with this gun business, but this
cuts deep. Every so often I scrape my hands into the
pocket, tracing the note's edge. It reassures me that
all of today's events were real. It's like a scab I can't
help but keep picking.

I've never felt so alone.

But I'm not. I hear Marcel's voice. "Just as long as
you understand that you aren't untouchable."

"Thelonius, you all right?" Mr. Blackmon drags
a chair over to my desk. He turns it around so
that he can rest his arms on its back. "You awful
quiet."

"I thought that's what you teachers wanted. As
long as we shut up and do as we're told, you collect a
check and feel like you've done something."

Mr. Blackmon purses his lips, the way a doctor

might when struggling to come up with a diagnosis. "This doesn't sound like you."

"Just leave me alone." I fold my arms and stare at my desk.

"Is this how you want to operate: anyone who sticks around, you show them the door?"

"Nehemiah's hurt because of me." The words tumble out of my mouth before I can catch them. Accidental truth, letting people know what you are actually thinking, is another rookie move.

"You want to tell me what's going on?" Mr. Blackmon performs his trick again. Most teachers ask a question but can only wait a second or so before they answer it themselves like they're afraid of the silence. He waits. And waits. He lets the space where I am supposed to answer grow until the silence demands a response.

"No." I manage to say.

"Oh, that's right. I forgot. If you talk to me, folks will think you're snitching." Mr. Blackmon checks over his shoulders in exaggerated precaution. "Some of them may be watching us now."

"Mr. Blackmon, seriously, why are you always up in my business?"

"I can't afford cable, and this is all the entertainment I have." He tips his water bottle to his mouth.

I attempt to cross my arms even harder to let this dude know to move on. If he won't take the hint, I'll have to go all in. "You know, there's been something I've been wanting to tell you for a long time. These little heart-to-hearts aren't as helpful as you think."

"I'm sorry you feel that way."

"I mean, is there a class you teachers take or something? Trying to be relatable to students?"

"Let me let you in on something: we're told to be what they call friendly allies. Supports that you feel safe coming to."

"Let me let you in on something: you just so extra. I have a mom. I have friends. You don't need to be either. So a little less friend and a bit more ally."

"Fine."

"Fine."

Mr. Blackmon scoots away from me. He's hard to read. I can't tell if he's upset, about to pout, or get in his own feelings. He hovers over his desk like he's thinking about something. I close my eyes to clear my head a bit. I may have been harsher than I intended. After a few minutes, he circles around to the desk behind me. Maybe he wants a better angle to watch the rest of the class. With his notebook open, Mr. Blackmon speaks in a low, conspiratorial whisper. "You know, I remember when I was in seventh grade. . . ."

"Didn't you hear me?"

"I heard you. I'm not talking to you."

"Is this going to be one of them old people stories?"

"I'm only thirty-two. And like I said, I'm not talking to you." Mr. Blackmon makes a show of flipping through his papers.

"Who you talking to, then?"

"Not you. We wouldn't want anyone thinking we talk. Anyone could just pop in. And I wouldn't want anyone to get the idea that we might be friends."

That stung more than I thought.

As if on cue, the door opens and Brionna strolls

in. She pauses at my desk, turns her head away from me as if she sniffed something foul, and wanders to Mrs. Horner's desk. She tosses her meds back in a quick swallow, grabs the remote, and flops on the couch. Once the screen burns to life, Twon and Rodrigo immediately sandwich her.

"Now that See No Evil, Hear No Evil, and Speak No Evil are all accounted for, I can keep going." Mr. Blackmon buries his nose in his paperwork. "I'm not going to run a line of bull by you. I had a dad. Big dude. His hand was the size of my butt. I know because he spanked me. Once. Most times he only had to give me that look and I knew he meant business. He and I were never close, not in the way I wanted. We didn't talk. He didn't know anything about me. Not the music I listened to, not the books I read, not even the teams I was into. It got to where I thought not only didn't he like me, but somehow, by the very fact of me being born, I inconvenienced him.

"On the other hand, however, I did have a teacher, my Sunday school teacher actually, who did take an interest in me. He was into comic books and horror movies and basketball. Things I'm into even today."

"Uh-huh," I say absently.

"Who you think keeps Rodrigo supplied with comics?"

"So you trying to pay it forward or something? 'Cause you know, this story's really touching me." I tap my heart. "Right here."

"Yeah, that was starting to sound corny to me, too, but you know I can't stop once I get going." Mr. Blackmon glances up from his notebook. "But seriously. I heard you. You're right. I do try a little too hard because I want you all to know you have someone on your side."

"I think we get that. You just need to give us room to do our thing, too. Some of this we have to figure out on our own."

Mr. Blackmon lets that sink in for a minute. "Anyway, you may be interested in knowing that Nehemiah's grandmother is coming to pick him up from the nurse's office. He'll be all right. His wrist may be sprained; otherwise, all the damage was just bruises and scrapes. Strictly superficial."

170

"I was supposed to have his back, but . . ." My voice trails off before anymore accidental truth slips out.

"I know you think you can't tell me what's going on. Why Nehemiah got jumped. Why folks are giving you the stink eye. Perhaps you know a bit more about the . . . situation than you let on." He halts just long enough to see if I betray myself with a reaction before pressing on. "I know things have been tense in this place lately, but not everyone is against you. You need to know you have people you can talk to. You have caring folks around you. Mrs. Fitzgerald. Your mom."

"You?"

"Let's not get crazy now." Mr. Blackmon closes his notebook and fiddles with his water bottle. "But even if you can't trust anyone grown, you do have something else going for you."

"What's that?"

"You're smart. Try and hide it all you want behind being cool or bored, but you are. So be smarter than your problem. Whatever, or whoever, it is. If they're bigger, don't come at them direct. Outmaneuver them."

"And if they're smarter?"

"Use your weakness as a strength. And don't let them see you coming at all."

With everything that's gone down, I'm so deep in my feels I can't think straight. But I have to if I'm going to solve this. Moms got me into reading Walter Mosley's Easy Rawlins books. I've started a list of guiding principles: think objectively and follow the evidence; think creatively and about every possibility; and never fall in love with your favorite theory. They help me begin to sift through the puzzle pieces so that they make sense:

- Marcel probably knows who did it but enjoys watching my head spin too much to say anything. A gun isn't her kind of play. It risks her getting her hands dirty.

- I don't care what Marcel insinuates, I can't see Nehemiah, Twon, or Rodrigo doing this.

- Pierce is a wild card, but this doesn't seem like a move he'd make.

- RaShawn has a motive, a couple in fact. He might have been wanting to settle up with Nehemiah. Either that or wanting to fend off or even take over Marcel's operations.

- Which leaves Kutter. This is right in his wheelhouse. Especially if he wants to take his menace routine to the next level.

It's already Wednesday and I can't help but think that I'm still missing a key piece of the puzzle. I could use a witness of some sort.

The stress must be getting to me. I have a head-ache that feels like construction workers ripping up my skull with jackhammers, so I stop by the nurse's office to grab an aspirin. I wait behind the counter walling off Mrs. Carson from the students. Mrs. Fitzgerald enters from the rear shadowed by a set of parents whose faces are somewhere between wor-ried and angry. She holds the door to her office open to let the parents go in first. Rather than locked-in lasers, her eyes have a faraway look to them. She moves like all her muscles are sore. With a deep inhale and slow exhale, she closes the door behind her.

"Mrs. Fitzgerald looks tired," I say.

"Yeah, you'd think the gun was found here at the school. Her last few days have been a nonstop whirlwind of meetings, phone calls, and parent con-ferences. Parents wanting to make sure their kids are safe." Her eyes meet mine. Not quite blaming me but making sure that her words land firmly. She lowers her eyes like she can't stand to look at me.

Maybe I'm reading into things.

My head throbs even more.

I try to ride out my day until my favorite part, Discovery Time, a time to choose our own activity. I always pick the playground. Without the rest of middle school out there, I walk the line. It's a favorite punishment of teachers: have a kid walk the painted line surrounding the basketball court while everyone else enjoys recess. It drives kids nuts being forced to walk while watching their friends have fun.

It was different if *I* wanted to do it. Walking is peaceful. Relaxing. It takes me out of my day, right before the chaos of the end-of-school routine, and it gives me time with my thoughts before I have to go back to my neighborhood. I drag myself to the classroom door as the clock winds its way to 3:00 p.m. Here I am with my chief suspect, Kutter, dogging me, setting us up to go down for his stuff in only a couple of days.

Once I return to class, the Special Ed class lines up behind me. Absently toying with the pencil sharpener, I brace against the wall and wait for Mrs. Horner to dismiss us. Her last act of the day, it reminds us that she holds the final bit of power over us. It doesn't matter to me since I'm not in a hurry to roam the halls.

Mrs. Horner motions toward the door. Mr. Blackmon marches us out the door. Most times he barely shadows us, respecting that we are middle schoolers and can find our own buses. We enjoy our increased sense of independence, looking forward to it since we dreamed about it when we were in lower school.

"You all right, Thelonius?" Mr. Blackmon asks.

"I'm cool. Why?"

"Normally you'd be almost racing out of this joint. Jumping, trying to touch every arch and overhang between here and outside."

"Just tired, I guess." Me and Nehemiah are like brothers. With so many people in our lives who let us down, we swore we'd be there for each other. Words are easy, I guess. When they got tested, really tested, I froze. Abandoned him, our friendship, like everyone else did. The guilt slows my steps. I walk in Mr. Blackmon's shadow, but not really alongside him. I don't bother to high-five any of my boys, not that anyone offers a hand. I don't clown anyone, don't try to push up on any of the girls. I scan the hallways, not sure what I was searching for. No, that's a lie. I watch for Marcel's grin. Or Kutter's threatening approach. Or any crowd of kids. Even mild-mannered folks gain courage in a pack, like a group of hyenas. Not quite in full creep mode, I skulk along. Not scared, there's a difference. I don't want it to appear like I am hiding. I'm not going to give them that satisfaction. Not my fear. "You all right? You normally don't walk us all the way down to the buses?"

"I just want to make sure there are no more . . . misunderstandings. Like with what happened on the basketball court."

Misunderstandings. So that's what the cool kids are calling it.

"Who you like now?" A girl's high-pitched accusation rises above the chatter of the hallway. My ears perk up at the familiar voice. Kids shove their way to the rear of the school, where the buses line up like goldfish waiting to be fed. I match a face to the voice and find the twins. I uptick my chin to Mr. Blackmon and head toward them.

"Nobody," Tafrica protests with a little too much strength.

"Lies and deceit!" Wisdom yells. "Then why you walking like that?"

"Like what?" Tafrica stops midstep.

"Like you trying to mop the floor with your behind. Look at you, swinging that thing."

"Girl, you fried." Tafrica begins walking again, her butt having a modest twitch with each step. It's hard to not notice once that level of attention has been drawn to it.

"I didn't say it. I'm just repeating what I heard," Wisdom says.

"Who said it?"

"Deja." Wisdom mutters half under her breath like she doesn't want to give up her source. Thing is, she's compelled to tell you how she knows things so that you know her information is solid.

"Which Deja? Tall Deja? Skinny Deja? Deja the Queen? Cockeyed Deja . . ."

"That's mean. No one calls her cockeyed Deja."

"But you knew exactly who I was talking about, didn't you?" Tafrica says.

Pausing on the bus steps, I glimpse Kutter. The boy forms a gun with his fingers to shoot at me. Careful not to meet anyone else's eyes, I slip into the bus and skulk behind the twins. No one joins me on the bench. The twins continue chatting away. A folded piece of paper colored with hearts and stuff sticks out of Wisdom's planner. They've been passing notes. Wisdom's a little paranoid: she never throws notes in the trash. From what I hear she either takes them home to throw away or stores them in a keepsake box. I dip my head forward as if trying to hear better, but stumble into them. They don't notice me palming the note.

"Why you in our mouths?" Tafrica rears up on me. Wisdom mirrors her neck swivel.

"I'm not. I'm just listening," I say, withdrawing before my exposed head makes too much of a tempting target for hungry lionesses.

"Like we your personal show or something." Tafrica's voice rises with a hint of disdain. Not directed at me, only enough to mount a fake protest.

"You're everyone's personal show. That's the way you like it," I say tentatively, hoping to navigate this minefield.

"Wouldn't have it any other way." Tafrica relaxes in her seat, satisfied.

"We need to be up on YouTube. Have our own channel," Wisdom says.

"Mm-hmm. We'd be famous."

"Million hits easy. Go viral."

"Triple OG low-key to the max," they say and slap hands.

With them distracting each other, I have a chance to read the note. They start off asking the same questions I have been about who brought the gun to school, except they talk about "that one," someone they suspect. I underestimate how exhausting it can be keeping up with the back-and-forth of the twins. I rub my neck. Tafrica was the harsher of the two, but has the ability to read people like a magazine. Wisdom is more plugged into what folks are saying, but left to her own devices is all rainbows and bunnies. I don't even know what I need to ask them, much less how to go about it. Tafrica lightly elbows Wisdom in the side and nods in my direction. I stuff the note into my pocket before I can read much more.

Wisdom squints, then crinkles her nose, almost making a stink face. "Look at you being all mopey."

"He probably wore out. All that 'not being there for your boy' can wear a body out," Tafrica says.

"I'm out." I scoop up my stuff as the bus nears the first drop-off. Two stops before mine, near the entrance of my housing addition. Me and Nehemiah sometimes step off here to race the bus to my house. I throw two fingers in a peace sign. "Deuces."

"This ain't your stop," Wisdom says.

"I could use the exercise," I mutter without meeting either of their gazes.

"Me, too." A smile spreads across Tafrica's face, like a shark who's caught the scent of chum, and she gives a slight chin wag in my direction.

Wisdom turns from her. "Yeah, you right. Some exercise might keep you from having so much behind to drag all over the place."

Ignoring them, I walk the aisle. The bus driver notes us disembarking, as if doing a mental catalog in case she has to make an incident report later. A half dozen sixth graders exit at the same spot. I raise my backpack to let them scurry off to their houses like rats caught in the light of the pantry. Soon it's just me, Tafrica, and Wisdom with a long stretch of sidewalk to my place.

"Saw what you did at recess," Wisdom says.

"What you didn't do," Tafrica corrects.

"You don't know what you saw," I say, a little too defensively.

"When it comes to that trifling boy, I suggest you break wide," Tafrica says.

"Nehemiah's my dude," I say.

"Who's talking about Nehemiah?" Wisdom says.

"He fried." Tafrica taps her head.

"But he isn't trifling." Wisdom wags a scolding

index finger at her.

Tafrica rolls her eyes. "Well . . ."

"He isn't. You need to quit."

"Who you talking about, then?" I ask.

"Kutter," Tafrica says.

"If you follow him, you heading right into trouble," Wisdom says.

"I'm trying to figure out why Kutter got it in for me," I say.

"Well, rumor has it," Wisdom begins, "that you started nosing around other folks' business. Like you're trying to put together a case on them. You know how folks get out here about that."

"Them who?" I protest.

"RaShawn. Kutter." Wisdom pronounces the names all solemn, like she's reciting a memorial for fallen friends. "Maybe a couple of others."

"You out here snitching on your peoples?" Tafrica blurts out and stops short to measure my response. "Makes it hard for us to trust you if you out here running game on your peoples."

"I. Ain't. Snitching. On. No. One. And I'm about

tired of having to defend myself. You know me. This whole neighborhood knows me. I'm as true as they come. I'm just out here, minding my own business, not *in anybody's mouth*." I half snarl, aiming the comment at Tafrica. We all have a code that we choose to live by. I'm no snitch, but I'm not going to hide whenever I see something wrong. One way or another, I'm going to figure out what happened and make sure the right person gets in trouble. "Just doing my do, chilling with Nehemiah. Next thing I know, suddenly I got beef with everyone. Got the principal bumping her gums at me. Mrs. Horner. Mr. Blackmon. You two. Kutter."

"No need to get all excited." Tafrica backs down, sounding somewhat pleased with how heated I got.

"You so combustible," Wisdom echoes. "We just needed to hear you say it."

"And look you in the eye when you did it." Tafrica starts walking again.

"I know who's behind all my troubles," I announce.

"Who?" Wisdom asks.

"Marcel."

Tafrica sucks her teeth. Then spits.

"Hate much?" I ask.

"We just don't have much love for Marcel." Wisdom hitches her backpack higher on her shoulder. One of her blond braids falls into her face and she brushes it back.

"She too wretched. Thinking she better than everyone else," Tafrica snaps. "She walk like she bowlegged and pigeon-toed."

"Bowlegged *and* pigeon-toed? That don't make no sense," I say.

Tafrica squats down to imitate her version of Marcel's walk. She circles us a few times, like a person with their knees on backward.

"The way the park always be jumping, someone had to have seen something," I say.

For some reason, Tafrica gets it in her head that Marcel's walk resembles a duck. So she lowers even more, tucks her arms in, and flaps them while quacking. Wisdom ignores Tafrica as best she can, waiting until she waddles almost out of earshot. "Someone did see something." Wisdom avoids my eyes. "You know who you need to talk to?"

Tafrica quacks.

"Who?" I ask.

"Jaron."

"Why Jaron?"

Tafrica quacks twice.

"That's on you. Assuming you really aren't out here snitching." Wisdom swats Tafrica on her passing behind. "Quit it. You too foolish."

"Stanky booty," Tafrica says.

"You fried, too."

Having instantly lost interest in me, the girls dart off, caught up in their own arguments. I mull the name over. Jaron. Judging from the jarring shoulder bump at recess, Jaron has no love for me. He may be still too raw from music class a couple days ago. But Jaron and Nehemiah were boys from way back, and I realize that I can't do this alone.

I need my brother by my side.

I remember how I first met Nehemiah.

It was back in second grade. Me and Moms had just moved to town. I was new to the school and new to the bus, so I stayed to myself a lot. I purposely chose the seat above the wheel. It shortened the seat, leaving no room for anyone to sit next to me. The constant rumble allowed me to drift in my own thoughts. A couple of middle schoolers kept kicking the back of my seat. They started jeering and cracking jokes, just in case I hadn't noticed their antics. I didn't need to turn around to know who was doing it. Their brand of obnoxious was its own fingerprint.

Tim Jackson and Jeff Eastridge. They exited a stop before mine, all hyped up.

"This isn't your stop," Mr. Miller, our then bus driver, said to Tim in his gravelly rumble of a voice. He had his gray-tinged black hair tucked under a baseball cap most of the time. He seldom spoke, much less shouted, even when Tim and Jeff had worked everyone into a near mob.

"My mom told me to stay with Jeff until she got home from work, Mr. Miller," Tim said, his fake innocence fooling no one. Blue eyes within wrinkled sockets glanced back at me, but Mr. Miller let them exit anyway. The bus slowly lurched forward. The two immediately ducked behind the bushes and ran for the next stop, only two blocks away.

The bus slowed down as it neared my house. I drew in a sharp breath, ready to race the final gauntlet to my house. My chest tightened. A familiar dull ache began in the pit of my stomach. My heartbeat climbed into my throat. I tried to swallow, but my throat squeezed shut. The boys managed to keep a lead on the bus, since it had to brake at each stop sign. The bus slowed for the last drop-off. My house.

"Mr. Miller's a caterpillar. Mr. Miller's a caterpillar," Tim and Jeff chanted.

The stragglers stepping off the bus joined in the pair's taunting. Everyone except me.

The chorus slowly stopped when the bus drove off. Tim and Jeff cornered me. The cartoony grins of their mouths grew so large, reminding me of hungry clowns, because they pressed in so close.

"Hey, lookee here, Jeff," Tim said. "It's our friend, Spear Chucker." Tim stood a full foot taller than me. His red hair shone to near orange in the sunshine. Freckles dotted his face so thickly at times, he wasn't too much lighter than me.

"Yeah, Spear Chucker." Jeff was my height and hadn't lost his baby fat. His chubbiness made him all the more ridiculous when he tried his tough guy routine. Thing was, he was actually tolerable when he wasn't around Tim.

"So, Spear Chucker, why don't you just go back to Africa?" Tim says.

"Yeah, Africa." For them, Africa meant the other side of town.

I calculated the distance to my home. It was a seven-house dash, but they'd never let me escape with a straight shot. A creek divided our neighborhood addition in two and ran through my backyard. A thick stand of trees separated the properties. Great for hiding, but if I got caught back there, no one could see them beat the snot out of me. Fueled by fear, I gambled that I could cut through the edge of the trees and jump the narrow part of the creek to make it to my back porch before they could reach me.

As Moms often says, I suffer from "big mouth, small behind syndrome." Luckily for me, my speed made up for the checks my mouth couldn't cash.

"Hey, Jeff," I finally said, "is your brother Humphrey back yet?"

"What brother?"

"Oh, I saw your mother on the corner last night yelling 'hump free.'"

Jeff lunged, but I slammed my books into Tim and took off. I jumped over the white wooden fence that surrounded the nearest house and tore through the yard. Panic already shot me off my plan. Still, they were going to have to work for this butt whupping. I wished I had an older brother, someone to look out for me.

While Tim gained on me, Jeff struggled with the fence. The yard was fairly small, and bushes taller than me lined it. An oak tree grew near the bushes, a path I'd mapped during a previous chase. I scampered up the tree without missing a step, climbed past the bushes, and leaped. Landing hard, I tucked into a roll. Moms was going to be upset when she saw the state of my clothes.

I ran behind the garage of the next house to escape the stares of my good-for-nothing classmates. A Doberman strained against its leash when I darted by. A church faced the street that bordered our neighborhood. I'd have to double back to make it to my house. I would be better off waiting them out.

I climbed down the stone-lined basement steps of the church and hid. I waited for the boys to pass noisily by. If they were to peer over the edge of the steps, I was cornered. After a few minutes, I held my breath, and peeked above the concrete wall of the steps. The boys headed down the road. I jogged back down my street. Some of the straggling kids shouted as I passed. Tim and Jeff turned only to see me standing on my front porch. Home.

Later that day, the doorbell rang. Three times. I hated it when people pushed the button more than once as if it were there just for show. When I yanked the door open, this little kid with his shirt only half-tucked in reached into his backpack to hand me my forgotten books.

"You dropped these." Nehemiah picked at his budding Afro.

"Thanks." I left the door open while I wandered into the family room. The kid couldn't have been too bad. He did bring my books for me, so I figured I owed him. Plus he looked like a stiff breeze could carry him off. Closing the door behind him, he followed me. I plopped down in front of our old television set. It was almost time for *Yu-Gi-Oh!* "You want to stick around? My mom just popped out to the store, but she'll be back. She'll make us some sandwiches."

"Sure. Then I have time to show you these." Nehemiah took several comic books from his book bag.

"Oh, man, you don't buy any of that crappy DC stuff, do you?"

"DC? Heck no. I wouldn't waste money on that crap. I got *Black Panther*, *Hulk*, *Luke Cage*, *Fantastic Four*, *Avengers*, *Thor*, and *X-Men*."

I picked through the stack. "How'd you get all these?"

"I skip lunch and use my lunch money."

After a two-hour block of cartoons, Nehemiah was still on the couch. Moms hinted around about him going home, but Nehemiah dodged the issue every time. She resigned herself to fixing dinner for three, but insisted on a phone number to check with his folks first. After a few minutes on the line with them, she stared at our phone like it was an alien tongue trying to lick her. She told us that she wasn't in a rush to drop him off.

"What do you want to be when you grow up?" Nehemiah asked.

"I don't know." I flipped through the channels,

bored with everything. "Maybe a cop or something."

(I have a theory that every boy goes through a cop phase. I'm certain mine was due to the amount of cop shows Moms watches.)

"I want to do something great, you know?" Nehemiah's voice faded off. "Something where I can be rich and famous."

"Wouldn't it be cool to have superpowers?" I interrupted.

"I guess." Nehemiah's hands fidgeted in his lap. His elbows were ashy. He never quite met my eyes when we talked. He'd either stare past me like he was focused on something just over my shoulder or study the carpet.

"I mean, if I had my choice, I'd be big and strong, like the Hulk. And no one would be allowed to pick on anyone smaller than them. I'd protect all of them."

"I'd choose flying. I'd fly all the time." Nehemiah almost looked directly at me when he said that. "When you fly, you're free."

I knew right then that I'd found my brother.

★ ★ ★

The next day, we were out at recess. Nehemiah and I chilled out by the kindergarten double doors. For all the time we'd been in class together, it was the first time we'd ever hung out at school. Some middle schoolers milled about during their Discovery Time. I spied Tim on the monkey bars. He teased some girl. She squealed, telling him to leave her alone. It sounded like a cry of help to me, so I trotted over there.

"Quit bothering her," I said.

"Mind your own business, Spea—" Tim checked himself since we weren't alone.

Not that it mattered. Just knowing that I wasn't by myself anymore made me see myself different. I was sick of him calling me names. Leaping up at him, I grabbed a hold of his dangling leg. Unprepared for me to lunge at him, he overbalanced and tumbled right off the monkey bars. It had rained overnight and the grass was still damp. The girl held her hands to her horrified face.

"You're. Dead." Tim brushed himself off as he

stood up. Jeff hopped up from the nearby picnic table to back him up. I found myself boxed in.

Nehemiah used a rubber band to shoot a paper clip at Jeff. It hit him just above the cheek and left a bloody slash as well as the beginnings of a welt. Cupping his face, Jeff barked in pain. His face flushed red, as if caught in a steam blast. Jeff charged toward Nehemiah.

"You're both dead!" Jeff wiped his bleeding cheek.

The two of them chased after us like twin lions about to pounce on a herd of sleeping gazelles. Nehemiah followed my lead. We ran from them, but not at full tilt, only fast enough for them to keep up. I wanted to lead them away from the girl. Once I thought back on it, I don't think she was in any actual trouble. They simply teased each other the way boys and girls who liked each other do. But I'd already committed, even though I had no real plan for dealing with them.

On the other side of the playground, an area of wet, worn grass glistened. A glimmer of an idea formed.

Motioning to Nehemiah, I changed directions, Tim and Jeff close behind, and headed toward the muddy grass. As my lead foot hit the fringes of the mud slick, my traction gave. I silently cursed my cheap shoes. Nehemiah wasn't faring much better. Tim and Jeff were dangerously close behind him, but he was locked into this gambit. We wobbled from side to side. Then I quit running. Instead I gave into the terrain and sort of slid across the top of the slick. Nehemiah reached out. I steadied him as he did the same thing. Sparing a glance to check our lead, the trailing duo never quit running. Greedy, Tim reached out toward Nehemiah, who had slowed down. His sneer gradually collapsed once he found himself slipping in the mud. His outstretched hand wavered, even grabbed after Nehemiah a few times before he went down. He latched on to Jeff. The more he tried to regain his balance, the more off-balance they became, until Tim pulled the two of them into the cool embrace of the mud. They flailed about in frustration. The rest of the class ran over to make fun of them.

The teachers came over to yell at us. I told them about them picking on me, on us, and the name calling (the adults were horrified by the words they called me). But we still got in trouble for instigating that fight. Tim and Jeff weren't problems again. In fact, they went out of their way to be nice to us for the rest of the year. At first I thought that they were playing up their innocence for the teachers to let the heat die down and then really get even with us. Every day we got off the bus ready to be chased or ambushed.

But nothing came. Not a name call, not so much as a lunge in our direction, not a gesture to make us flinch. They were the next two families to move out of the neighborhood.

Nehemiah has been my dude ever since. I had to do something to make things right between us.

12

It's hard for me to be patient when there's so much going on. Even if it's just in my head.

Sitting on my couch, I flip through the television channels, not really paying attention to anything in particular. I'm not sure if my mind can't focus or if I just want to distract myself. I know what I need to do, but to put my plan into action I have to wait on Moms. Of course today she wasn't already home to greet me. Finally the key jostles in the lock. Ahrion bounds into the room. She doesn't understand how big she's getting. If she does, the realization doesn't stop her from a running start and leaping onto the couch to tackle hug me.

"Want to play video games? I have a new racing one," Ahrion says.

"I'd love to. When I get back, okay?"

"Where are you going?"

When I stand up, I make sure Moms isn't watching us and I pass Ahrion a pack of Twizzlers. She loves the stuff, but Moms limits her candy intake. I press my finger to my lips.

Ahrion touches her lips with her finger and then promptly yells, "Moms, Thelonius gave me some Twizzlers!"

"Thelonius, you know better," Moms scolds without any heat.

"Sorry, Moms." I bend over to Ahrion. "You're the worst at secrets."

I'm careful to smile at her so that she recognizes that I'm kidding.

"I know." She jumps up to hug me. "I'm the worst."

Once I untangle myself, I slink to the kitchen. "Moms, can I ask you something?"

Something about the way I ask the question,

maybe my tone since I was trying to let her know I was serious, causes her to freeze. She turns off the stove and gives me her full attention. "What is it?"

"I need to go over to Nehemiah's." Moms doesn't like me walking over to his stretch of the neighborhood. All those cop shows she loves watching so much convinced her there was a serial killer or child molester behind every bush. I quickly laid out my case. "I won't stay long. I'll call your cell when I get there and right before I leave so you'll know when to expect me home. And if I spot RaShawn, or his sister, I'll make myself scarce."

"Why? Did something happen? I was wondering why he wasn't here." Moms tilts her head, examining me.

I hesitate. The word catches in my throat and I barely squeeze it out. "Yes."

"Want to tell me about it?"

"We . . . had a fight. I need to make things right with him." My eyes brim with the beginnings of tears but I refuse to let one fall. I plead with them, hoping she'll see that I have to do something, this one thing, on my own.

Her eyes soften. "All right, but be careful."

The entrance to our housing addition serves as the dividing line of the entire neighborhood. The subdivision mirrors itself along the main street. It cuts through the houses like a giant smile, all the courts and lanes branching from it. What was worse was that only the main street had a sidewalk running alongside it—even then, just on one side. Moms is pretty good about giving me space to do my thing. Though she gave her permission, once or twice along the way, I swear I spot her cutting through people's yards to keep a watchful eye on me. I keep waiting for Ahrion to leap out of a stand of trees and yell "Here I am!"

I want to be more independent and all, but I hate coming over to Nehemiah's. It isn't because I have crossed some invisible dividing line and suddenly find myself in a bad area of town. That's how so many people react whenever the idea of coming here pops. Actually, it's because whenever I spend time there, I'm struck with an overwhelming sadness.

Nehemiah's house is a brick-trimmed, cream-paneled, two-level home. Our housing addition only had two floor plans to choose from: our ranch style and this one. Weeds grow too high along the building's side. I ring the doorbell twice and step back on the porch. The curtain covering the door pane flutters. A lone, careful eye checks me out before the curtain falls back in place. Finally the door opens.

"Hi, Mrs. Johnson. Is Nehemiah here?"

"You know he is. Where else he going to be?" Mrs. Johnson is a dragon, but also Nehemiah's grandmother. She wears misery for makeup and chugs bitterness for vitamins. Nothing is ever done right or satisfies her. She tugs her gray sweater tighter around her like she suspects I might attempt to mug her. "Who are you?"

"Thelonius Mitchell, ma'am." I hate the way she never bothers to remember my name, as if I'm beneath her notice.

"Don't 'ma'am' me. Showing up on my doorstep, looking all raggedy. You the one that got Nehemiah into all that trouble, right? I saw you down at the school hiding behind that teacher like he was your momma's skirt." She dangles her hand out like she's clutching an invisible cigarette.

"Can I talk to him?" I lower my head and kick at the loose rocks along the doorframe.

"Now you trying to ignore me like I ain't even here? *I'm* talking to you. *I'm* the one whose day got interrupted to come see about Nehemiah."

"I'm sorry, ma'am."

"Yeah, you are." Mrs. Johnson slams the door so hard that the knocker clatters against it and the frame shudders.

I jump at the sound and remain on the porch, not certain what to do next while the thud echoes. My mouth twists up. I nearly swallow my lower lip while I debate on whether to knock on the door again. Voices rise on the other side of the door.

"I *wasn't* being rude. I just don't have time for foolishness. Yeah, he still out there looking all pitiful," Nehemiah's grandmother says to a voice I barely make out. "Like I care what some boy who still smells like his momma's milk thinks." She pauses again. The curtain shivers. A loud huff follows. The door opens, Nehemiah's grandmother's backside walks away from me. "Come on in here, boy. I ain't got all day to mess with you."

I putter behind her. The inside of the house stirs even more sadness. The house suffers from neglect like no one cares about anything and anger has seeped into the walls. Scuff marks scrape the dingy and chipped paint. Holes in the plaster have been mortared over in crude swatches when covered at all. Chunks are missing from the ceiling tiles. Cracks splinter the doorframes as if they had been kicked in once or twice. The trim around the bathroom door shifts loose. The carpets, which once had been green or tan, are worn to a dull gray.

"Why'd you come around here?" Nehemiah meets me at the end of the hallway, cutting me off from the rest of the house. A bandage wraps his wrist.

"To make sure you're okay," I whisper.

"*Now* you worried?"

The words sting, but I deserve them. Perhaps a part of me still hopes that Nehemiah didn't see me freeze. Didn't see the fear on my face. That Nehemiah doesn't know what it feels like to be completely alone, abandoned even by his best friend. I think that's part of the reason I had to come. To hear Nehemiah yell at me, saying what he needs to say. He turns on his heel and stalks into the next room.

"Well, well, well. Look who decided to come down from the mountaintop and pay a visit to little ole us." The source of the mystery voice who kept yelling at Mrs. Johnson is Nehemiah's mother, Rhianna. Shimmying down the stairs, she acts like she's not that much older than us and wants to be seen as cute. Not too much older than Nehemiah—she should still be in college or something. I have to admit, she is kind of pretty. Most times, though, she just seems tired. I can almost hear Moms's voice say that Rhianna can't make up her mind which person she wants to be:

1. a young woman with a dream she doesn't know how to make come true. She still has time to go back to school, get a job, get her own place; she just needs to act like a grown-up.

2. a young woman who wants to forget
   she has a kid and live the life a girl
   her age should be living. Her world
   should be all parties and boys.

"This visit can't make your moms happy." Rhianna always acts as if there is some beef between her and my mother that I can't possibly understand. It's on both sides, since Moms hates for me to be around her. The two of them all but growl whenever they near or mention each other. "You looking to get my boy in more trouble?"

"No, ma'am. I came over to apologize. To you and to him."

"Oh?" She moves toward the kitchen to get a glass, wandering about, deciding what to fill it with.

"Yeah. I haven't been a good friend. Haven't stood up for him like I should. I already spoke to Mr. Blackmon about how the fight on the basketball court was my fault, not Nehemiah's. And I brought his schoolwork so he won't be behind."

"You want something to eat, baby?" Rhianna

riffles through their cabinets. "Nothing fancy like what you and your moms have all the time. At least to hear the way Nehemiah tells it. Probably why he's always staying up by you all so much. We do have them microwave pizzas and fries."

"I love pizza." It never occurred to me that anyone thinks we live high and fancy. Or that we believe we are better than anyone, especially Nehemiah. I wonder if we are seen as putting on airs. I don't know. I'll leave that one for everyone else around me to figure out. All I care about is my friend.

I slump down on the couch next to the chair Nehemiah's curled up in. A series of fine lines, where the glaze no longer held up, stress the mismatched lamps stationed on either side of the couch. I grab a cushion and hold it in my lap. Frayed at the edges, they have been turned backward to hide the tears in their fabric. Nehemiah has already changed into a pair of shorts, showing off his ashy knees. He works a screwdriver into his toenails, to pick them clean.

"You hear all that?" I ask.

"I guess." Nehemiah doesn't glance up from his toe-jam operation. "You ain't falling in love with me or no mess like that, are you?"

I hadn't realized how tense I had been. Every muscle tight, braced for a punch. With that single comment I could breathe again. A smile fills my voice and I slowly begin to relax. "You need to shut it."

The two of us enjoy a brief silence, as much as there is to be had with the clanging of the microwave door and the banging of dishes. What I like most about me and Nehemiah is that we don't have to talk. We just understand each other.

Under the glare of the forty-two-inch flat-screen, bought with their tax-refund check, Rhianna's boyfriend shifts on the other couch. Sprawled out, and too tall for the sofa, he tries to make himself comfortable.

"What's up with that?" I whisper.

"Man, I don't even know. I don't bother to learn their names anymore. You know what he had me do?"

"What?"

"Pee in a cup for him."

My eyes widen in disbelief. "For real?"

"Yeah. Talking about how he was up for a job and didn't want them to bounce him if they did a drop on him and he came up dirty."

"You do it?"

"Charged him twenty dollars."

"Won't the tests show that he ain't been through puberty yet?"

"Can they test for that?" Nehemiah's voice rises with sudden worry.

I shrug. That's the sort of stuff that Moms doesn't want me around. "Hood nonsense" she calls it. I don't know. It's just folks doing their best in a rigid system.

Rhianna brings in a tray of pizza slices and French fries. We quit talking as soon as she walks in. "What were you boys talking about?"

"None ya." Nehemiah smiles.

"What?" Rhianna sets the tray down in front of us, freeing her arms.

"None ya business."

"Boy, don't make me remind you who you talking to." Rhianna stops in her tracks and narrows her eyes at him, a warning that he neared a line he better not cross.

Nehemiah flinches. "I was just playing."

"Me, too." Her frown broadens into a warm smile. She presses his head to her chest and kisses the top of it. "I'll leave you boys to your boy business."

I pick the pepperonis from my pizza and stack them next to it. I eat the remaining cheese slice with gusto. Leaving the crust, I pop the pepperoni bits into my mouth one at a time. Nehemiah eats with his elbows out like he's guarding his plate, gobbling his food as fast as he can shovel it into his mouth. Without asking, he grabs the crusts from my plate.

"Act like you've seen a meal before," Mrs. Johnson yells from the kitchen. "You ain't in prison. Yet."

Nehemiah leans forward, as if somehow he was out of his grandmother's earshot, and speaks in a conspiratorial whisper. "What did I miss in school?"

"It's like the entire vibe at the school flipped on

me." I explain about the snitch rumors, emphasizing that they fell on me alone. How I spent the rest of the day ducking folks, spinning it like I was some secret agent wrongly accused, having to dodge assassins at every turn. Nehemiah takes it all in. He taps his chin thoughtfully with my pizza crust.

"So where are we at?" he asks. "My money's on RaShawn. The gun was found by his spot. And assuming he wasn't *that* level mad at me, he still might think he needs it."

"What about Kutter?"

Nehemiah cradles his wrist at the sound of the name. I hang on the seat arm. "He always wanting to show everyone how thug he is. Like it's some Boy Scout badge or something. Marcel tried to get in my head, telling me to watch those closest to me."

"Who? Rodrigo? Twon?" Nehemiah shakes his head. "Nah, I don't see it."

"That's what I'm saying." I ease back into the couch.

"What if we're going about it all wrong?" Nehemiah sits up with a sudden thought.

"What do you mean?"

"What if it wasn't a student at all?"

"What makes you say that?"

"When I was in the nurse's office, a delivery dude buzzed the office to get in. How many people come through, drop stuff off. Mailmen. Parents. Shoot, RaShawn's sister if he forgets his lunch."

"I . . . hadn't thought about that." *Think creatively and about every possibility.* The possibility resets the game. A whole new pool of suspects springs to mind. "The twins wanted me to talk to Jaron."

"You want to go near anywhere they send you?"

"Maybe he's some kind of witness. If he ain't come forward, it's 'cause he's scared."

"That makes sense. He don't want to be labeled a snitch. Or definitely would be afraid of pointing the finger at a teacher."

"Either way." I lick my fingers. "I don't know Jaron except to mess with."

"He all right. He's been tripping lately. Like he's two people and you never know which one you'll meet from day to day."

"I was thinking we try to talk to him tomorrow. You know the dude. He might still feel some sort of way about me after the music room thing." I turn away and mumble, "Not that I blame him."

Nehemiah stabs at his last bits of pizza. He refuses to make eye contact with me.

"You *are* coming back tomorrow, right?" I press.

Nehemiah raises his arm to examine his wrist. "Might as well. Don't see what the point is, though. Ain't nothing much for me."

"What do you mean?"

"Look around—this is all I got. This is all that's waiting for me. I don't believe much in tomorrows."

I twist away from him because meeting his eyes hurts me in the bottom of my stomach. I wish I was older or smarter and had all the right words to say.

"All I know is that I can't solve this without you." I hold my hand out. For a heartbeat, Nehemiah just stares at it as if making up his mind. Then he grins. We clap our hands, fire our guns, and snap our fingers. "I guess I'll have to believe in tomorrows enough for both of us."

"How did it go?" Moms asks when I walk through the door.

"You mean over at Nehemiah's?" I examine her, hoping to catch her out of breath or sweating from running after me. "It was okay."

"You know I'm not real fond of you going over there."

"But he's my friend."

"I know, baby." A hint of sadness fills Moms's voice. "But there are . . . influences I want to keep you away from. Life shouldn't have to be so real for you already."

"It's real all the time for Nehemiah."

"And if I could, I'd keep him from those influences, too." Moms hugs me. For a long time. Hard.

"Are you going to let go?" I mumble from her chest.

"In a minute. I got something to tell you, and you're not going to like it."

"What is it?" My head mushes into her side and I can barely breathe. I try pulling away, but

Moms grips me tighter in her now less-than-tender embrace.

"Mr. Blackmon called. He wants to meet with the both of us in the morning to discuss your recent behavior."

I fidget in my seat, never quite finding a
position I'm comfortable in. The Ed room seems
different. Quiet. Too quiet. Neat. Alien. Every afternoon once the students depart for the buses, Mrs.
Horner stays behind in order to straighten up and
reset things for the next day. I did the same thing
with my bedroom. Having everything in its place
relaxes me and gives me a sense of control, even
against the futility of a mess being made of it all
over again the next day. Since Moms couldn't drop
her off before the meeting, Ahrion finds the box of
Legos and quickly fixes the cleanliness and quiet
problem.

"Did you hear about yesterday?" Mr. Blackmon asks.

"Bits. What I managed to drag out of him and piece together," Moms says.

"Good, so he doesn't just do that with me." When he puts that bass in his voice, it always sounds like he's almost flirting. Mr. Blackmon flashes a toothy grin.

"Every conversation is a battle."

"I'm right here, you know." I'm bored of swiveling back and forth, so instead I position my chair between them. When grown folks start talking about me like I'm not in the room, more times than not, they are figuring out how to team up against me.

Having built two cars, Ahrion revs her engines.

"I just wanted to make sure everyone was brought up to speed. With all that's been going on—the gun, the fight—things can get forgotten. Slip through the cracks, as it were, if we don't stay on top of them. I wanted to give us the time and space to talk about how some of these things may be affecting you." Mr. Blackmon's voice takes on that special quality, of his warning me that he's about to invade our feels.

"You the school counselor now?" I ask.

"I just feel, and correct me if I'm wrong or out of line, Mrs. Mitchell"—Mr. Blackmon faces her before turning his attention back to me—"like you're walking along a precipice, Thelonius."

"A what?"

"Press piss," Ahrion yells from the Lego pile.

Mr. Blackmon stares at me. "A cliff's edge."

"Why didn't he just say cliff?" I ask Moms.

"Thelonius." Moms pats me twice on my thigh to settle me down.

"It's like you're trying to walk as close to the edge as possible. I wanted you to see that you don't have to go it alone," Mr. Blackmon says.

"What's your deal?" I ask.

"You're really hung up on that," Mr. Blackmon says.

"Everybody has a deal."

"Some angle they must be working." Mr. Blackmon says it like it's a question.

"Exactly."

"What's mine, then?" Mr. Blackmon lowers his

hands into his lap, daring me to come at him.

"I don't know. That's why I'm asking."

Mr. Blackmon scoots back in his chair and inhales deeply. He pivots back and forth for a moment. I recognize the body language. Mr. Blackmon's trying to figure out the next way to approach me. "You're a good kid, Thelonius. I don't know if you hear that enough."

"Excuse me?" The way a rattlesnake shakes its tail as a warning, Moms's "excuse me?" alerts everyone that she's about to bite.

"Moms caught you slipping," I say with a wide grin.

"Believe me, I know you hear it from your mother." Mr. Blackmon remains focused on me; his smooth delivery doesn't waver. "If any of us thinks otherwise, she's quick to let us know."

Moms straightens in her seat. "Dignity and pride. I teach my boy to walk upright, with his back straight. There's none of that sagging pants nonsense around the house. He doesn't let anyone strip him of his dignity. Not the school. Not his friends.

Not the neighborhood. And not himself."

I shrink in my seat. I don't need to actually be here. It's embarrassing. Their expectations are a lot to live up to. I want to tell them that I'm not trying to get kicked out of school. That I especially want no part of being transferred to Banesford Accelerated Academy. That I dream—when I let myself dare to dream—of doing something . . . smart in life. Like be a scientist, to figure out how things work. Maybe be like one of those detective scientists on television who solve crimes. That would be so lit. No one would see me coming.

But most times those kinds of dreams seem like they're the future for someone else. I hear the voice of Mrs. Horner making fun of me. Kids like me don't become scientists. That's not even worth dreaming about. I'm a screwup. I'm going to let them down. Those voices may be right, but . . . I don't know. I'm not ready to give up on it just yet.

"So it's with that in mind, a student came forward to say that she heard you brought the gun to school."

Marcel. No, not her. I mean, I know that she's behind it, but she would've put someone else up to it. Not Kutter, because Mr. Blackmon said "she," and besides, no one would believe him. Someone more low-key. Brionna, maybe. "That's the rumor. It's what Mrs. Fitzgerald all but accused me of from the jump."

"Did you call us in here to ambush us with accusations?" Moms is about too through with this conversation.

"The opposite, actually. We're still looking into things, doing a thorough investigation. No one's going to move on rumor. I wanted to give Thelonius an opportunity to tell his side."

"Look, Mr. Blackmon." I meet his eyes, then Moms's. "I'm a little extra. I get that. But this is next level. I didn't do this. There's a lot going on in the school, things I'm still learning about. But this situation, it isn't on me."

"You know I believe you, T. You know better than to have me out here looking foolish defending you if you did it. That said, I got you," Moms said.

"You're a good talker, Thelonius. I knew I needed to hear you say that. But you need to know that if you are all talk and no action, then all you are is empty air. And I know there's more to you than that. I want you to step up some more. Take on more responsibility. Get you to fight for what you believe in, and, should that flame get lit, fan it to make sure you keep fighting. You have so much potential and could be a powerful leader wherever you go." Mr. Blackmon reaches for his water bottle to allow time for his words to settle in before continuing. Even he has to realize he's just laid it on pretty thick. He turns toward Moms. "It takes a lot of voices speaking into a child's life, fighting for them, in order for them to turn out okay. And, Mrs. Mitchell, I wanted you to know that I'm on your team. However I can support you, I'm here."

With the two main adults in my life batting life lessons at me for each other's benefit, it's time to derail this nonsense. "Are you hitting on my mom?"

Ahrion's engines go silent.

"Thelonius!" Moms yells.

"You are, aren't you? I ain't going to just sit here and let him push up on you. Talking about how much he cares, like he's trying to be my dad or something." I admit, this would be the corniest flirting I'd ever seen.

"Is that what you think?" Without fluttering an eyelid, not seeming flustered in anyway, Mr. Blackmon swigs more water. He just looks at me—through me—in a, I don't know, paternal way.

Ahrion smashes cars into each other. Lego pieces fly everywhere. Ahrion giggles as she begins rebuilding them.

Crossing my arms, I lean away. There are times when a dull ache pains my belly from missing my dad. After school or on a Saturday afternoon, the back of my mind itches like there's something I forgot or was supposed to be doing. Throwing a football with someone. Playing video games with someone. Having someone to show me stuff. I imagine it's similar to, like, having an arm missing: it may have felt real all the same, but the pain was in my head.

"I still think you need a pet or something."

Mumbling, I shift toward the window.

"Fair enough." Mr. Blackmon smiles. The eight o'clock bell rings. Ahrion jumps. "Want to give me and your mom a minute to go over your work to date? I promise I won't hit on her."

I study Mr. Blackmon carefully with something shy of a stare down. Before I escape, Moms tugs at my arm to bend me low to kiss me. I wipe it off but smile. Nehemiah and Twon walk in together, trailed by Rodrigo, who nips at their heels with constant chatter. I step away from Mr. Blackmon's corner to join them by the cubbies.

"What's that about?" Nehemiah glances back at Moms.

"Surprise parent-teacher conference," I say.

"You in trouble?"

"Always."

Nehemiah waits for Twon and Rodrigo to wander to their desks. "I saw Jaron. Told him we wanted to get with him at recess."

"Good. Maybe we'll finally get to the bottom of things."

We are the brotherhood of the flinch.

One way or another, we carry that fear with us. Every one of us. You can see it in the eyes of folks when you walk the school hallways. Always on guard. Always on the lookout. Never knowing where the next hit might come from. Never knowing who might roll up on you. We live in a state of shock, being worn out from always having to be on guard 24/7. We live with that sense of resigned relief when the punch finally lands and we think "at least now it's over" until the cycle starts all over again. Sometimes it's playful. Nehemiah wants to make me jump, and I have to live with never knowing when I am going to get caught slipping. There are other times, though, like the way Nehemiah flinches at his mother's touch. Tiny, almost imperceptible, it would have been easily missed, but I saw it.

The flinch.

Brushing off Nehemiah's hand clap on the shoulder with an exaggerated sense of bravado, Jaron plays off him, flinching with a shrug.

"Don't sneak up on me. Never sneak up on a brother," Jaron says.

"My bad. Didn't realize I was in full creep mode," Nehemiah says.

"I'm just saying. I'm a beast."

"All right, all right." Nehemiah holds his hands up.

The way Jaron scans the recess playground tells me a different story. I've never seen this side of Jaron. Actually, other than noting him being a big dude, I'd never actually "seen" Jaron before. Up until now, Jaron's just been another nameless plaything. Some dudes just have "mark" written on them and you just have to mess with them.

Still mad about being provoked into blowing up in music class, Jaron keeps his back to me, an intentional disrespect, which I let stand without saying anything. He probably had a session with Mrs. Fitzgerald and a detention day or two. It wouldn't take a genius to piece together that I wound him up on purpose. I was just messing with him; it wasn't personal. He was in the wrong place at the wrong time when I needed to vent. I mean, I'm sorry he got caught up or hurt or whatever, but he had to see that he wasn't the only one I gassed that day. I can't figure out the words to say and it's not like we're going to hug. That's not how we do things. I can't show softness and neither can he.

The silence builds between us until it demands an action.

I shift noisily and clear my throat. Jaron rotates on his heel, slow and deliberate, until he faces me. A mild sneer crosses his face. He stares me up and down as if I'm small. "What you need? Nehemiah says you wanted to talk."

"Why you so mad? I do something to you?" I play ignorant to draw out Jaron's thoughts.

"I just don't like . . ." Jaron breathes hard through his nose. His face twists a bit like waves of conflicting emotions hit him all at once as he searches to attach a name to one of the feelings that trouble him. Resentment. Being used. Feeling burned by a supposed friend. I can only guess. I give him a chance to name them, because I'm sorry for them all. "Nothing. Forget it."

"Look, dude, I'm sorry about the other day. I got you in trouble in music class. It was a . . . misunderstanding." I glimpse Nehemiah waving me off. "Anyway, I been letting a lot of folks down lately and I needed to step to them like a man and apologize."

"For real?" Jaron's large shoulders relax, if only slightly. His walls lower, if only a bit. "Yeah. We cool."

I swoop on the opportunity to press in a bit. "Look, I was talking to some folks. I was having a problem with Kutter and they sort of pointed me your way."

At the name, Jaron's face lights up with full interest. "What sort of problem?"

"He came after me. Except he didn't come direct. I think he went after Nehemiah to send a message to me."

"What did he want with you?" Jaron asks.

"I don't know."

Jaron arches an eyebrow with skepticism and distrust. His eyes harden about the edges. His walls prepare to rise again.

"I have a theory, though." I scramble to keep Jaron open to hearing me out and talking. "I think it had something to do with Marcel."

"It always does." Jaron wipes his palms along his pant legs.

"I'm not even sure what I did to rub her raw." I chance a step closer to him.

"You get in her business?"

"Not really. Just let her know that I knew."

Jaron laughs, a dry, bitter cough. "You might as well have threatened to make a run at her. She's paranoid. And ruthless."

"That how you got on her radar?" I ask.

Jaron starts telling his story, which might as well have begun "once upon a time. . . ." I picture his story in my mind as he speaks, a scene opening with how . . .

. . . *the sun beamed down on them from a clear sky. School had been in session only a few weeks, but the way the warm days kept coming, summer threatened to never end. The playground was a roiling sea of red or navy blue polo shirts and khaki shorts. The sixth-grade teachers struggled to wrangle their students, still not used to the discipline of the school routine. The middle schoolers poured out of the double doors, erupting onto the courts with yelps and furious intent. Ms. Erickson had recess duty. She swung a set of jump ropes with a sixth grader as Brionna traded off with some of the girls doing double Dutch. A substitute teacher wandered the periphery of the basketball court, making time to chat up Mr. Blackmon. He hovered about, not daring to take his eyes from his charges who walked the line.*

Three teachers covered the playground, but the

playground can be a large place, full of shadows. For those who knew how to stalk, there was plenty of room for predators to hunt.

A group of girls stood in a semicircle. The twins held court at the double doors as if they couldn't wait for recess to be over. An alcove over by the kindergarten wing of the building hid another set of double doors. Like the main double doors, no one could enter without a key card, but Marcel haunted its shadows, keeping a careful eye on the recess activities. From her vantage point, she couldn't see the domain of the gossip girls: the swings or the picnic-bench area where clusters of girls congregated to gossip. However, she could see the basketball court and, more important, the games that went on behind the mammoth playground equipment.

The massive fort divided the yard: wide ramps, steel decks, a maze of tubes, an enclosed double slide, a bridge that led to a tower, and a rock wall. All recycled plastics surrounded by a mat of wood chips and cut-up bits of tires. Safety first. Behind it was a whole other world as kids could play as rough as they wanted out of the sight of the teachers. Only the screams of raised ruckus drew any notice.

Marcel smoothed out her khaki skirt. Her mother insisted on her wearing a white blouse rather than a polo shirt. The look helped her play her part. Dutiful daughter. Prize student. Unlikely hawk. A lollipop dangled from her lips. She monitored her business. Candy sales, mostly, money changing hands. She had five boys selling for her now. With Kutter making sure all funds managed to get where they were supposed to.

Enter Jaron.

His parents prepaid his lunch enough for a single meal per day, but Jaron was a big boy who enjoyed his share of snacks. Wanting to duplicate the success Marcel had with her entrepreneurial enterprises, he took the birthday money his grandmother had given him and invested it in candy. There was a specialty candy shop over in the Lafayette Square Mall and he bought candy not found in Dollar Tree. He charged more than any of Marcel's sellers, but his was a premium product. Soon he found himself flush with *cash, cutting into Marcel's then-budding racket. Placing him firmly in her sights.*

"How's business?" Kutter eased up to him. He growled more than spoke, and his words had the ominous cast of storm clouds. The boy couldn't even ask about the time without it sounding like a threat.

"I'm doing all right," Jaron said.

"You know this is my yard, right?"

"It's a big playground. There's room for all of us." Jaron smiled. Innocence was a dangerous thing. He genuinely believed that there was a big enough pie for everyone to get a slice and be happy.

He underestimated how much some people enjoyed pie.

Kutter knew how to use his size. He stepped into Jaron's personal space, making sure the intrusion wasn't lost on the bigger boy. Kutter was smart, an eager student of Marcel's, and was careful not to lay a finger on Jaron. "It's not as big as you might think. There's only room for one candy dealer out here."

"I . . ." Jaron began to backpedal, away from the weight of Kutter's hot breath, but stopped when he bumped into RaShawn right behind him. "I get it. I'm through."

"That's not good enough." Kutter patted his pockets. "Now see, my pockets feel kind of light. If only a good Samaritan could help me out."

"How about . . ." Jaron tried to hide the stammer that crept into his voice. "I give you ten dollars? Would that help you out?"

"That it? That's not very charitable." It was Kutter's turn to smile. It was ugly and jagged, like someone took a broken bottle and carved a slit where a mouth should be.

"How much would . . ." The question died on his lips. A wall of boys gathered, cutting them off from all prying eyes. He knew how this dance was meant to end. He began to dump out the sandwich bag he'd tucked his money into, but Kutter held his hand out. Jaron placed the entire bag into his greedy palms.

Kutter turned to Marcel. She shook her head.

"Here's the thing: here at Persons Crossing Public Academy, we employ a teaching method that's part lesson and part practice." Kutter attempted to imitate the voice of Mrs. Fitzgerald. It would have worked, if she had laryngitis, fake gold fronts, and halitosis. "We like to foster a sense of community and leave no child behind."

RaShawn tittered.

Jaron's attention went from Kutter to RaShawn to the boys crowding in on him back to Kutter.

"What does that mean?" Jaron stammered.

"It's recess. We're about to play a game and we don't want to leave you out."

"What game?"

"Liftoff."

Kutter grabbed Jaron under his right arm, RaShawn under his left. As Jaron struggled, two more boys grabbed each of his legs. The boys held Jaron aloft and powerless no matter how much he wriggled. He yelled, begging them to stop. To put him down. Calling for his mom. The boys achieved a full gallop, running in a circle, and drawing a crowd of curious kids. Their cheers drowned out Jaron's cries.

One of the boys carrying a leg stumbled, losing his grip. Once that leg hit the ground, the boy on the other leg released his burden. Jaron dangled from Kutter and RaShawn, his dragging legs kicking up rocks and wood chips, leaving a sputtering dust cloud in their wake. Kutter and RaShawn counted off.

"Three, two, one . . . Liftoff!" Kutter and RaShawn yelled in unison and let go.

Jaron went tumbling forward. His body crashed into the ground, his momentum spilling him behind over head. All to wild peals of laughter and screams.

"What's going on back here?" Ms. Erickson yelled, drawn by the suspicious crowd and noise.

"Nothing, Ms. Erickson. We're . . . just playing," Kutter said.

Jaron stood up slowly, swept the wood chips from his pants and shirt. The stains on his pants smeared further with each swipe. He brushed tears from his face. The dust on his face blurred into a sad, muddy streak.

"You all right, Jaron?" Ms. Erickson wrapped a concerned arm around his shoulders.

Jaron's eyes went from Kutter to the crowd of faces

waiting to see what he'd say, back to Kutter. "Yeah, I'm good. We're just playing."

"Well, play nicer. Your parents spent good money on those clothes and I'm willing to bet they don't want to see them torn up." She paused, not quite buying their act. "You sure you're okay, Jaron? You look a little shaken."

"I don't feel well. I think . . . it's something I ate."

"You all play too rough, especially so soon after lunch. Go on to the nurse's office."

Jaron hung his head low, not wanting to meet anyone's eyes. Embarrassed. Ashamed. Angry. Scared. A swirl of feelings surged in him all at once, each one a punch to his belly threatening to send him to the dirt again.

That was Day One.

Marcel decided to make an example of Jaron. A continual reminder of what it would cost someone to cross her. Jaron never knew when something would happen. Cornered in the bathroom. Isolated or, worse, surrounded, at lunch. The constant whispers and taunts. Or in the park, where there weren't *even any adults within earshot should things get out of control. When he was truly on his own. Despite his size, the boys were emboldened, especially if there were four or more. Jaron lived with the fear. With the constant undertow of threat.*

He lived in the flinch.

With dawning realization . . .

I think back to my own actions, provoking Jaron just because I was upset. Something ugly twists in my belly. I find that I can't meet Jaron's eyes. I'm no better than them. At my bullying, Jaron had snapped. Determined not to take it anymore, he charged across the music room. I know the answer to the question before I ask.

"Jaron, who brought the gun to the park?"

"Thelonius, you don't understand what it's like. You all but run this place. Who's going to mess with you?"

"You'd be surprised." That was the lesson Marcel wanted to teach me. That anyone can be messed with. "Jaron, who brought the gun to the park?"

"Thelonius . . . don't make me say it."

"I have to hear the words."

"I . . . I was so afraid. The more dangerous you seem, the more likely they are to leave you alone. With it, I had the power for a change." Tears stream down the big boy's face. His hand, which seem too small for his body, wipes away his tears. I hate seeing big people break down, but it has to be done. I have to know. Jaron fishes into his pocket. He holds out his fist and waits for me to open my palm to receive its contents. When I do, bullets rain into my hand.

"I didn't even know how to load it," Jaron whispers.

Judgment day has come.

Nehemiah passes me a note. Mrs. Horner's in a particularly bad mood, probably because by the end of the day, Mrs. Fitzgerald is due to pronounce sentence on all of us, including her. So this class time has been designated a "silent working period." It's kind of like playing the quiet game except that the first person to talk gets sent to the principal's office.

So what's the plan?

Nehemiah writes in his barely legible scrawl.

We need to clear our name, but Jaron
is one of us. Right?

We're ride or die.

The only one who should go down for this is Kutter.

Not Marcel?!!?!!?

Nehemiah adds more exclamation points and question marks than necessary.

I'd love for her to go down for anything.
Her breathing should be grounds for
the Scream Room because she's taking
perfectly good air from someone else.

I hear that.

I'm working on something. But first things
first: we have to get out of here.

Like any good prison story, sometimes there has to be a great escape. And sometimes the simplest route, right out the front door, is the easiest. Life is all about waiting for opportunities to present themselves. Or creating those opportunities with a nudge here and there.

Try as the system might, we don't make good drones. Those "good" kids, the ones that fall immediately quiet when the teachers flick the lights off, the ones that line up perfectly when the teachers raise their hands and count backward, they're always going to fit in. Nothing wrong with that. We just come at the world different because it comes at us different. It comes hard, we go hard. We don't fit in with how the system wants to define us and sometimes we have to turn the system on itself for us to get by.

Pierce sits at a back table, away from the array of student desks arranged four by four in front of Mrs. Horner. His head ducked low, he focuses on his construction project. I should be the last person guilty of writing someone off, but I've never really taken the time or interest to watch him in action before. Granted, a dust mote floating by is usually enough to distract him, so most schoolwork is a struggle for him to get through. But give him some drawing pencils or paint and paper and he's locked in like a laser. Along his desk are paper cranes, sharks, and butterflies, since origami is his latest fixation.

> You could wind Pierce up. He can keep everyone distracted for days.

> No, I need to do better. But I think you're onto something.

I take out a new sheet of paper to begin a note to him, but think better of it, in case there's a repeat of me sneaking someone something they want but shouldn't have and getting low-key reported for it. Instead I wait until Pierce and his overly polite self asks to sharpen a pencil, and I linger at the cabinets searching for a book until he gets there.

"Hey, Pierce," I whisper while my back is to Mrs. Horner.

Sheer panic covers his face. Pierce scans about, one, to make sure I was talking to him and, two, to make sure Mrs. Horner doesn't see him talking. I'm under no illusions: Pierce is difficult to reach on his best days. Connecting with him is like journeying to another planet and you know your universal translator is on the fritz.

"No worries. I'll chat. I was wondering if you ever had any bad dealings with Kutter."

Pierce jumps at the name, a full body spasm like I'd just punched him. With his flinch I get another queasy feeling that, for better or worse, Pierce is part of our brotherhood. And we should take care of our own.

"It's okay. He's done it to me, too. To all of us. We want to stop him. Are you interested in helping us?"

A light flickers in Pierce's eyes. It's like watching part of him climb out of a deep hole he'd chosen to crawl into. He gives a barely perceptible nod.

"Good. We just need a small distraction. Something to get Mr. Blackmon out of the room for a little bit. Nothing that would get you in trouble."

Pierce nods. I'm not a real big fan of the weird smile he wears on his face.

By the time I get back to my seat, Pierce reports to Mrs. Horner's desk. My heart skips as he turns back to me. My gut lurches on visions of giving Twizzlers to Ahrion. But then Pierce scrunches his face at me. I think that's what passes for a wink for him.

"Mrs. Horner, may I borrow the stapler?" he asks.

"What for?"

"To finish my origami project."

"Sure." Mrs. Horner hands him her stapler. "Be careful. It's touchy."

Pierce ambles back to his desk and proceeds to

finish his latest figure. He's constructed paper fingers, which he's slipped onto his hand. When one hand is fitted, they look exactly like razor claws. Pierce takes the stapler and lowers his finger into it. Once I realize what he's doing, I start to wave him off.

"Ow!" he yells.

Mr. Blackmon strolls into the room escorting Twon and Rodrigo. He directs the two to their seats and attends to Pierce without breaking his slow strut. "What happened?"

"I cut myself," Pierce says in a weak voice. He runs his hand through his hair, leaving a streak through it and a red smear on his face. "I tried to get my claws on tight."

"Let's go to the nurse's office." Mr. Blackmon grabs a couple of blue forms. Medical reports. "I'll be back, Mrs. Horner."

Mrs. Horner nods from her desk without glancing up.

See? One down.

I pass the note back to Nehemiah.

This was your plan?

More or less. Pierce is always good
for a distraction.

What about Mrs. Horner?

I motion back to Twon.

Do you think you can convince those two to
cause a ruckus? They already have at least
one infraction, though. I don't know if they
can afford any more without it leading to
detention.

No worries. If I can get on Mr. Blackmon's
laptop, I can unflag them without any problem.
The system won't issue a detention.

How?

Please. I've had his password from the first
week. Mrs. Horner's, too. Memorized they
keystrokes. Even if I didn't, Mrs. Horner keeps
hers in her middle drawer.

Remind me not to unlock my phone
around you.

Too late.

Can you get word to them?

I got this.

Nehemiah is like a coach when it comes to ruckus. The squad looks to him to call a play, and with a hand signal or two, they line up in formation. I barely catch his gestures, much less a non-paying-attention Mrs. Horner.

"Why you got to always talk about my momma?" Twon jumps up.

"What? I didn't say anything," Rodrigo protests.

"You got to keep running your mouth."

Rodrigo backs up. "I swear, Mrs. Horner, I didn't do anything."

Twon pounces on Rodrigo. Grabbing him in a headlock, he wrestles him to the middle of the floor. He holds Rodrigo for a minute, then whispers into his ear. With only a hint of a smile, Rodrigo begins to fight back, but none of the blows land with any real feeling. Like brothers, Twon and Rodrigo fight often, since no one can push Twon's buttons like Rodrigo. Also like brothers, the two of them have each other's back more times than not. Mrs. Horner resigns herself to leaving her seat to intervene.

"What is going on today? You two are going to Mrs. Fitzgerald's office. Nehemiah and Thelonius, before you get it in your heads to act up, report to Ms. Erickson's room."

"But we didn't do anything." I almost sound like I mean it. I definitely deserve an award for this performance. Though Twon's act might give me a run for it.

Mrs. Horner's breath stinks and when she glides out from behind her desk, she talks too close to a person's face. "You're not in trouble, but I can't leave you alone. Don't ruin my trust in you to make it down there on your own."

"We'll be okay," I say.

"Is Brionna in on it, too?" Nehemiah asks as soon as we're out of earshot.

"Nah. She likes to run her mouth too much," I say. "This was the easy part of my plan. Now comes the hard part. You up for it?"

"Can't wait. What you need me to do?"

Education is a full-contact sport.

The students in Ms. Erickson's class crowd around books. They arm themselves with rulers and calculators like they were gearing up for war, not just checking their work. Another group huddles along the carpet in the rear as Ms. Erickson illustrates problems on a whiteboard. The excitement charges the room. I wonder if this is what it's like to be just another drop in the sea of different shades dotting the landscape of the room. A couple of girls wear hijabs, which shake as they nod in agreement with their teacher's words. The kid in front of me taps his pencil against his notebook. Studious gazes track Ms. Erickson's every move. It all feels so . . . normal.

"Today we're going to review percentages." Ms. Erickson walks between the clusters, more bird of prey than protective mother hen. I check the time. There are about twenty minutes left in fourth period. Lunch is up next. If I know Mrs. Horner, she'll wait until lunch to collect us and enjoy the extra moments of peace and quiet alone in the classroom.

Wearing a bored smirk, Marcel notices us as soon as we enter. "Ms. Erickson? We have some . . . visitors."

"What can I do for you fellas?" Ms. Erickson examines our hands for a pass or paperwork of some sort.

"Mrs. Horner sent us down here. She had to . . . step out," I say.

"I see." She rumples her face, weighing our answers, already planning to verify our story. "Can you handle quiet time?"

"We'll see," Nehemiah says. I elbow him in his

side. "I mean, yes, ma'am."

Nehemiah takes the desk by the front door while I make my way over to the opposite side of the room, at the rear by the computer station. An elderly woman who volunteers at the school three times a week raises her glasses to her face to get a better look at me. Sniffing with immediate disapproval, she screws up her mouth as if she smelled bad fish.

"Before we get into our lesson," Ms. Erickson announces, "we need to back up. We got off track this morning and have some catch-up to do. Thank you for shifting gears so smoothly."

Ms. Erickson waits for her students to settle into their seats. Without being told, they each take out a pencil and a sheet of paper. The discussion opens with proper and improper fractions.

"I need to see pencils moving. Stay focused," she exhorts.

The elderly woman picks up on her cue to patrol the room, helping anyone who seems to struggle to keep up.

Kutter leans his chair back, making a show of

not paying attention. He jabs one pencil into the eraser of another, making a two-tiered super pencil. He attempts, and fails, to twirl it around his finger. He sends one skittering across the room, but otherwise isn't too disruptive. Ms. Erickson obviously lets it slide in order to concentrate on those students who actually want to learn.

"We have seven minutes left until lunch and I want them all," Ms. Erickson says.

Even with my practiced academic appearance— my head buried in a book I only pretend to read—I know Marcel's watching. She measures each shift, each twitch, probing for any weakness to exploit. Searching for any hint of what I might be up to, because I *have* to be up to something. I smile. I can't help myself. When things are about to break my way, be it a good idea or circumstances lining up for me, I can't help but be pleased with myself. Besides, I'm not the one she should be watching.

I meet her gaze. Then nod.

"What happened to my pencil?" Nehemiah yells.

"What's the problem?" Ms. Erickson strides

toward him in long steps.

"Someone took my pencil!"

"Who?"

"Kutter." Nehemiah points.

Kutter freezes. His remaining pencil nearly completes a revolution around his finger but skitters to the ground. Already tilting back, he nearly falls out of his chair with the accusation. He raises his long arms in bewilderment. "Man, you tripping. How am I going to get something of yours from over there?"

"Stop playing and give it back," Nehemiah says.

"On my momma, Ms. Erickson, I don't know what this fool is talking about," Kutter says.

"Who you calling a fool?" Nehemiah stands up at his desk.

"You, fool." Kutter rises in response. "I didn't stutter."

"You want to bump?" Nehemiah steps toward him.

Everyone rises out of their seats, some to clear out of their way, others to get a better view.

"I ain't scared of you," Kutter says.

"You must be scared of a toothbrush, though," Nehemiah continues. "I can smell your skunk breath over here."

"Whoa!" the class murmurs.

"You must want to be split." Kutter tromps toward him. He flexes with each step, his movements like a snake uncoiling.

Kutter and Nehemiah face off against one another. Easily four inches taller, Kutter looms over Nehemiah. Not backing down an inch, Nehemiah shows heart, or is plain crazy. Ms. Erickson wedges herself between them. Sadly, every teacher in public school has seen this production a hundred times before. She spouts words encouraging them to settle down, take a breath, reminding them that fighting isn't worth it and that there are better ways to solve their problems. She escalates to threatening to call Mrs. Fitzgerald and then their parents if they fail to take their seats. Each one alternates chest puffing, half-lunging toward the other. The rest of the students congregate around them.

"You want to go?" Kutter asks.

"Whenever you want. I'm tired of all your crap," Nehemiah says without any real heat to his words, his voice on the verge of cracking. With laughter. He's enjoying himself too much and I don't know how much longer he can stay in character.

My plan puts me in a bit of a moral quandary, if you will. Not that anyone could tell, I'm in the middle of what some might call a crisis of conscience. I'm trying to do better, but I'm not sure what better looks like just yet. I think of it as using my powers for good against a bad guy. I already know that I may need to work on developing new powers, but until then, I'm going with what I know.

I inch toward the rear of the crowd, letting the elderly assistant brush past me as she moves to snatch one of the boys away from Ms. Erickson. I slide next to the cubbies. As everyone watches the pretend fight, each boy puffing their chests but doing little more than preening for show, I find Kutter's backpack and slip Jaron's bullets into it. Call me paranoid, but I'd wiped down the bullets and slid them into an envelope and used it to pour the bullets into his backpack. I make my way toward Marcel. With a resigned glint in her eye, Ms. Erickson backs away to grab a couple of reflection forms from her desk, ready to just send them both to Mrs. Fitzgerald. I had to give Ms. Erickson that much: she hates having to resort to reflection forms. She views them as a last resort and a failure on her part.

"Enjoying the show?" I whisper to Marcel.

"I've seen better." Marcel chews a piece of gum with the empty expression of watching clothes dry.

"It all comes down to the finale. Watch this." I wave.

Nehemiah screams and runs around the room. That grabs Ms. Erickson's attention. She dashes to cut him off. Her assistant moves toward the door. She might be old, but she can block an entrance and prevent a scrawny seventh grader from running down the halls like a madman. Nehemiah leaps over a desk to the oohs and laughter of the class. He reaches into one of the cubbies and started tossing things. He chances an approving peek at me. I motion at him to move to the next cubby over. Nehemiah grabs the next backpack and swats its

contents toward Ms. Erickson. The bullets jangle to
the floor.

"Ms. Erickson, are those real?" Nehemiah freezes
with the suspicious bag held away from him.

"You've got to be kidding me," Marcel says to me.

"Everyone back away. Give me some room," Ms.
Erickson says. The students retreat in a stunned
silence, stepping widely around any of the rolling
bullets. She turns to her volunteer. "In fact, can you
take them to lunch and send Mrs. Fitzgerald down
here? You can leave Marquess here."

I'm not used to anyone calling Kutter by his gov-
ernment name.

The volunteer cajoles the students into a line. "No
one touch anything."

Ms. Erickson stretches her arms out to stop us.
"Nehemiah and Thelonius, you stay here also."

"Why me?" I protest.

"I just know you're involved in this somehow."

I don't know whether to be insulted or impressed.
Because either even Ms. Erickson blames me when
things go down, or she saw through our little performance.

All lessons come at a cost.

An Indianapolis Metropolitan Police Department squad car squats out front of the school, its lights flashing. Kids press themselves against the windows to get a better look at it, like it was some new exotic animal at the zoo. The other students fill their doorways, ignoring the severe warnings of their teachers to take their seats. Bathroom passes run at a premium since suddenly everyone has to go at the same time. The hallways bustle with the few students allowed out, now burdened with being the eyes and ears of their classes, fully expected to come back with as many details as they can ferret out. They linger at the water fountains for any possible view.

A lone IMPD officer escorts Marquess Neal, aka Kutter, through the halls. Stragglers in the hall too close to the action flatten against the walls, afraid Kutter is patient zero and they might catch a case of being hauled to Banesford Accelerated Academy. Kutter stands tall, walking without cuffs, delivering the perp walk everyone expects. Mrs. Fitzgerald appears heartbroken. Rings settle around her eyes. With fine cracks around her lips where makeup had been judiciously applied, she stifles a yawn but pauses to stretch. With bits and pieces gleaned from careless whispers and carefully worded reports, she constructs a narrative to share with everyone.

The school assembly convening today would be about bullying as well as a discussion on school safety. Kutter was a bully. He terrorized all the kids at Persons Crossing Public Academy. In order to further build his rep, to take it to another level, he brought a gun to school. Not to actually hurt anyone, just scare them. Show them that at any time he not only had access but the will to bring it. However, Persons has a zero-tolerance policy. The school administrators removed the threat and would use this opportunity as a teaching moment. That was a story Mrs. Fitzgerald could sell. I muffle a thin smile at that. My way out was to provide and stick to this simple story.

"There was no need for things to go this far." Mrs. Fitzgerald folds her arms. "I'll give you one last chance to tell me why you did it."

Kutter stops in front of her. He faces her with that empty expression, eyes haunted by the ghost of having given up or given in to what everyone thought of him.

"Like you taught us: *S*ay the problem, *T*hink of solutions, *E*xplore consequences, *P*ick the best solutions." Kutter's dead and hopeless tone chills me. Inspecting me up and down, he glares at me with hollow malevolence. Mrs. Fitzgerald catches the stare down and guides me toward her office while the officer escorts Kutter to the cruiser.

␣␣␣␣*

Mrs. Fitzgerald has me stew outside her door while she deliberates. The waiting is still the worst part. The "go and think about what you've done" technique is standard for teachers and parents alike. In practice, it amounts to "worry about what kind of punishment you're gonna get."

I consider how long it has been since I've done an actual turn at detention, but my gut assumes that my detention-free days might be nearing an end. The wait allows my mind to play out every way the conversation might go. I come up with counterarguments and strategies. Should I plead for mercy? Play up being contrite? Go for pity? Cry? Go on the offensive with righteous indignation and anger? This is what they want: have us wear ourselves down with impotent worry.

Marcel walks into the outer office, brandishing a broad smile for each of the office assistants. She delivers some paperwork from Ms. Erickson. She twirls her hall pass around her finger like a prison guard playing with the keys for the cells while they count the inmates. Marcel's smile turns brittle as she faces me. Sliding into the seat next to me, she stares straight ahead.

"Getting your sentence handed down, Felonius?" Marcel asks.

"I'm not guilty of anything," I say.

"You don't honestly believe that, do you?"

"Then I'm as guilty as you," I say.

"If you truly believed that, then you have nothing to worry about. But here you are, looking all worried. Like they're going to haul you out the way they did Kutter."

"You ain't worried?" I ask. "About . . . anything?"

"That Kutter might turn snitch? Nah, I told him as soon as those bullets came spilling out that he wasn't riding with me."

"You're cold. You'd cut your people in a minute," I say.

"It's cute the way you think we're so different. I'm not worried about Kutter because he's a soldier. He'll stand tall because it's in his best interest. Even without copping to anything, the accusation hangs over him. Having the rep of bringing a gun to school will serve him well over at Banesford, if that's his fate. Just like it would have Jaron."

I rear back in my chair, but catch myself and struggle to regain my cool.

Marcel straightens a pleat in her skirt. "Don't act like that was supposed to be a secret. You know I hear things."

"I see you for what you are," I say. "Pure gangsta. You prey on and eat your own if it suits you. In the end, you're all about you."

Mrs. Fitzgerald's door opens a fraction, expectant, letting me know that she's ready for me.

Marcel knows to make herself scarce, leaving after one parting comment. "If I look familiar, it's because game recognizes game."

I accept her hat tip of respect, but she's wrong. I'm not like her. I won't be.

Mrs. Fitzgerald waves her hand for me to sit down. There's no play in her tired eyes.

"You can wipe that smugness off your face," she says without preamble.

"Why're you so mad, Mrs. Fitzgerald?" All my charm lands like a raw egg thrown at a wall: it splatters, useless, and slides down leaving a mess.

Mrs. Fitzgerald bridges her fingers in front of her. "You kids are so darn clever, aren't you? All of you think you're smarter than us stupid grown-ups. That we have no clue what pressures you're under, what problems you face. As if we've never been you or done all the nonsense you haven't even thought of yet. You're in seventh grade, Thelonius. You are twelve years old. You think that you have it all worked out."

"Times are different." Out of instinct, to lighten the mood, I almost make a joke about her age. Staring into her stony face, I decide to bite my tongue rather than risk riling her up any further.

"The more things change and all that." She sighs. "What am I going to do with you?"

"I haven't done anything wrong."

Mrs. Fitzgerald unfurls her fingers. She slaps the desk like someone struck with a good idea. Startled, I jump. "There you go again, being the smartest person in the room. Your mind is always ten steps ahead of your behind. Now I know you know everything, but our job—mine, your teachers', your mother's—is to see the big picture."

"I still don't see what this has to do with me."

"Here's what I think: though he's fully capable, I don't think Mr. Neal brought the gun to school. I don't think you did either. I *do* think Kutter has been a problem for a while."

"He a straight-up bully." The words leap out of my mouth, my heart eager for her to believe this.

"I'm stuck with the evidence and will have to think about his future here. I also think that you know more about what's been going on than you've let on."

"I ain't a snitch." I know there's some truth to it. There's a line I have to walk. I know Mrs. Fitzgerald and Mr. Blackmon. I like them. I think I even trust them. But they're still—I don't know—the system. I can't trust the system to do right by us. They created the prison; we try to live by prison rules. We have to protect our own. Do right by the community.

Me and Mrs. Fitzgerald lock in a chess match, but I hate the game. I've been told that I'd be good at it, but I never had the patience for it.

"I understand that. But you need to understand that no one in administration can do much unless we have help. Kids have to be willing to trust. To talk." Mrs. Fitzgerald sighs again. Scooting out of her chair, she paces behind her desk. "So you do things your way. Let's see how that's worked out: Pierce hurt. Rodrigo and Twon in detention for fighting. Nehemiah in detention for disrupting class. Marquess expelled. And with all of that, do you think we've caught all those responsible?"

I imagine Marcel's grin and say, "No."

"I don't think so either. But we can learn, even from our mistakes. How could you have handled the situation better? How could you have made some better choices?"

"We don't make choices, we make impulses."

"Your impulses." She paused. "Your actions put you and those around you at risk."

"When we got nothing but bad choices and poor

options in front of us we just do the best we can in the moment."

"We need you to do better."

"We need you to make a better world, then."

Mrs. Fitzgerald sighs. She rubs her face like she is tired. "You know, in your own way, you followed STEP, too. You said the problem and thought of a solution, and—I'm just speculating—all the subsequent shenanigans were your attempt at picking the best solution. You're more resourceful than I think you're given credit for. But, still, you didn't explore the consequences. So again I ask, what am I to do with you?"

"You've got to punish me." I hate the high pitch that crept into my voice.

"What for?" Her eyebrows arch in surprise.

"I . . . deserve it." I slump in my chair. I let down Nehemiah. I bullied Jaron. I'd gotten my people hurt or in trouble. My face flushes hot. I wipe at my eyes.

Mrs. Fitzgerald softens, as if she'd waited on this moment from me. "Here's what I think: you found out what was going on, but by not coming forward, you violated the spirit of the school's honor code. We value character in our leaders."

"I'm no leader," I whisper.

"Mr. Mitchell, a leader takes responsibility for the people they lead. A leader sees a problem and acts to fix it. You've highlighted some issues. We do need to do something different with you. I told you from the beginning that I was reassessing how the Special Ed room operates. It's a relic of the previous administration whose time I think has passed. What do you think?"

"What's going to happen to Nehemiah, Twon, and Rodrigo?"

"There you go again: worrying about your people first. I'm afraid despite your best intentions, you're shaping into a leader. What do you think we ought to do with you all?"

"Me?"

"Yes, you. If you were in charge, what would you do?"

"I'd transfer us back to regular classes." I thought about it for a little longer. "Maybe have Mr. Blackmon, I don't know, help supervise us in class."

"He does seem to understand your class well."

"He a'ight, I guess." I couldn't just leave him out. In a perfect world, he's not a complete pain to have around.

"As it so happens, I'm thinking through exactly that sort of reorganization. Starting the next quarter, you'll all be transferred back to regular classes. I picture the Special Ed room being more of a resource room. A place where students can go when they need extra support."

"Extra support?"

"More time to take tests. A pullout space for teachers to provide specialized help. A place where students can calm down when they get amped up."

"So one big Scream Room?"

"More like one big specialized study hall. I think we're squandering some of our most talented and creative assets. Do you know what 'squandering' means?" She winks at me.

"Yes, ma'am." I smile despite myself.

"I've got my eye on you, Mr. Mitchell. Tomorrow is another day and another opportunity to make better decisions."

Epilogue

Sometimes you have to find your victories where you can.

Nehemiah, Rodrigo, and Twon scramble about, playing army with Lego weapons. It's raining outside, thus our Discovery Time choices have been reduced to indoor games. Legos is always a popular choice, but Mr. Blackmon forbids us from constructing anything that vaguely resembles a gun. No Lego rifles. No Lego lasers. No Lego cannons. We manage with Lego grenades. Hurled correctly, the pieces splinter and fly farther about the room. Our version of army almost resembles dodgeball.

Mr. Blackmon only half pays attention. He's busy studying with Pierce. All I picture while watching

272

the two of them is Ralph Wolf and Sam Sheepdog. They each have jobs to do. The past is forgotten and today is a new day.

"You have ten fingers up in your face." Mr. Blackmon sits across from Pierce, wiggling his fingers. "Take away two and how many are left?"

"Too many." Pierce cradles his head in his palm.

"How many?"

"Eight." Pierce slams his pencil down on his desk.

"All right. All right. Next . . . you know what nine minus eight is."

"One."

"You know what? I shouldn't interrupt." Mr. Blackmon leans back in his chair. All Pierce needs is the proper encouragement. "You got this. Do it your way and knock it out."

I tumble onto the couch. Brionna hogs the remote, determined to watch the end of *The New Adventures of Pippi Longstocking*. What Brionna sees in that live-action Raggedy Ann–looking girl, I can't fathom, but it keeps her quiet. I perk up when RaShawn enters the room. Sullen and tired, he hands a note to Mrs. Horner.

Mrs. Horner sets the note on her desk and claps twice. "Okay friends, I need you to gather around for a special community circle."

Twon rolls behind the couch to avoid taking fire. A Lego grenade explodes behind him. Rodrigo and Nehemiah close in on him from both sides, intent on taking him alive.

"I have an award and treats to hand out as soon as everyone is ready," she says a little louder.

That cuts through the noise of war. The trio scoops up all stray Lego pieces in a flurry of motion. They fill out the rest of the couch, though Twon stations himself on the floor in front of me.

"I know last week was a rough week. We've had some ups and downs. More downs than ups, I'd guess. But I want to acknowledge our ups when they happen. Nehemiah, can you come over here?"

Nehemiah casts about, his body jerks like a puppet whose puppeteer had its strings tangled and can't get the head fully up. He drags himself over to Mrs. Horner. She presses him to her side.

"Nehemiah did some great work. He figured out what had been happening to our pens and pencils. When middle school recess and lunch are going on, the room is empty a lot of the time. Nehemiah pointed out that this had to be the time the thefts were happening. He suggested that I double back here from the copy room. Sure enough, I caught young mister RaShawn here, who had a pass to be on his way to the nurse's office, rummaging through the desks. So I wanted to present Nehemiah with a Citizen of the Week certificate to take home. He also gets an item from our Reward Store."

All eyes on him, Nehemiah exaggerates a pimp stroll to the picnic basket that serves as the Reward Store. He fishes about for a bag of Takis. When he walks by, we slap our palms and on the backswing, bump our back hands. As our hands clap again, we clasp thumbs and flutter our hands upward like wings. When we part, we press hands as if in prayer and bow to each other. We're working on a new hand-shake. He opens the bag back at his seat and swats away Rodrigo's hand when he reaches for a Taki.

"We don't tolerate theft or destruction of property here at Persons Crossing Public Academy." Mrs. Horner doesn't care about any of that. With the coming reorganization, she's strutting around like she's about to be paroled. "Hopefully you all can take RaShawn under your wing and help each other to a better way."

RaShawn's reception amounts to a series of resigned groans from the couch. He doesn't have that many friends and struggles to fit in like we all do. RaShawn's strictly a follower. I know the type. They latch on to whoever's the strongest, the smartest, the most feared, the most daring, and take their cues from them. Around here, that's me. The top sheepdog.

I cut them a glare that stops all the complaints. RaShawn pauses, a little unsure of us. Of me. I give him a nod. "We got you."

Stories are all about how they are read, not the teller's intent. Sometimes the intent and the meaning match up, but sometimes they don't. It's easy to let a bad story get in you and define you. To let that version of how people see you soak in and take root, growing inside you until you find yourself becoming and acting out that story. It's one reason I'm as suspicious of "teachers" as they are of me.

If we have to go through life as a suspect, we have to take victories wherever they come. That's the reality of our world. For now. Our journeys won't always be perfect. They may be downright messy, but it's all about figuring out how to get through life. We do the best we can. We look out for each other.

Maybe I am a spider.

Sitting motionless at the center of my web. Strictly chilling, because that's all spiders do when left alone. They go through their day, relaxing and minding their own business. But they're also smart. They do little themselves—they just plan well. They build elaborate webs to do the work for them to maximize their chill time. Each strand stretches out, connecting all over the place so that they know when something's going down even without them being right there. That's the thing about spiders—they deal with all the insects that truly pester people. So people who are afraid of spiders can't see how valuable they really are. Yeah, that can be my story.

Though, sometimes, I still may have to amuse myself.

Acknowledgments

For all those times the students I worked with asked, "Mr. Broaddus, is there something of yours I can read?" and I looked them in the eye, considered my portfolio, and said "no" (because your parents would kill me), the answer is now yes.

So, for the students and faculty at The Oaks Academy Middle School and the Snack's Crossing Elementary School, thank you for the inspiration and opportunities to work for you.

For the patient, guiding hand of my editor, Claudia Gabel.

For my agent, Jennifer Udden, since this is the project that began our relationship.

For all the librarians at ALA who encouraged me

to write this in the first place (a wise writer always listens to the advice of librarians).

For my sons, Reese and Malcolm, for whom the dynamic of Thelonius and Nehemiah (and far too many of their antics) should seem familiar. And, lastly, for my wife, Sally, who still lives in a state of complete denial about the "here's my neck" scene.

For all of you, and all those who've gone unnamed who have loved and supported me so well over the years, I say thank you.